8/11

The Quality of
MERCY

D1413302

ANNE SCHRAFF

SADDLEBACK
EDUCATIONAL PUBLISHING

URBAN
UNDERGROUND

A Boy Called Twister
The Fairest
If You Really Loved Me
Like a Broken Doll
One of Us
Outrunning the Darkness
The Quality of Mercy
Shadows of Guilt
To Be a Man
Wildflower

SADDLEBACK
EDUCATIONAL PUBLISHING
www.sdlback.com

© **2011 by Saddleback Educational Publishing**
All rights reserved. No part of this book may be reproduced in any form or by any means, electronic or mechanical, including photocopying, recording, scanning, or by any information storage and retrieval system, without the written permission of the publisher.

ISBN-13: 978-1-61651-006-0
ISBN-10: 1-61651-006-4
eBook: 978-1-60291-791-0

Printed in Guangzhou, China
0510/05-72-10

15 14 13 12 11   1 2 3 4 5

CHAPTER ONE

Alonee Lennox was lying on her bed, looking at old yearbooks from middle school. Her twelve-year-old sister, Lark, joined her.

"Alonee, that's when you were twelve, like me," Lark cried excitedly. "That's a cute boy standing there in the picture with you. You're dressed funny, in a long dress. And is he in tights? What was that all about?"

"Oh, we had like a fair from the Middle Ages," Alonee explained. "I was voted queen of the fair. He was voted king."

Lark looked closer at the four-year-old picture. "Wow, that's Jaris Spain. He was cute when he was twelve years old," she commented.

"Yeah," Alonee sighed. "He's even cuter now." There was a wistful tone to Alonee's voice.

"You like him, huh Alonee?" Lark asked. Lark was slim and pretty with large dark eyes and long lashes.

"Sure, I like him a lot," Alonee admitted. "We've been friends since we were both building block castles in preschool. He was the cutest little boy there."

"I mean, really, *really* like him," Lark said. She seemed to have an understanding beyond her twelve years.

Alonee shrugged. She never shared how she really felt about Jaris Spain with any of their friends at Harriet Tubman High School. Sami Archer, Trevor Jenkins, and Derrick Shaw were among her closest friends. But she never came right out and told any of them that she was in love with Jaris. Maybe they knew. Surely Sami knew. Not much got past Sami. But to tell them would have changed the friendship in the close little group. And what good would telling them do? Alonee always knew that Jaris loved Sereeta Prince. Even in middle school he would look at her with admiration. Now Sereeta and Jaris were dating regularly. There was never any doubt in Alonee's mind that her own feelings for Jaris went way beyond friendship and that his feelings for her stopped short of love.

"You know Alonee," Jaris told her not so long ago, "you're special to me. You're one of my best friends."

And Alonee had replied, "Sort of like a really nice sister."

Jaris quickly replied, "I didn't say that," but that's what he meant. That's all it ever was to Jaris—a deep friendship. He saved his love for Sereeta Prince. When Sereeta ignored him, he loved her. When Sereeta was in so much turmoil over her family problems that she scarcely noticed Jaris, he loved her more. He rushed to her side to help her. When Sereeta finally told Jaris that she loved him too, he soared into the sky with happiness.

"Well," Lark said, "you kind of love him, huh?"

"I love all my friends," Alonee responded elusively. She looked at the twelve-year-old boy in the picture, at his the dark, dreamy eyes, at the half smile curving his lips. She saw the vulnerability that was always there. Her heart did a little leap inside her. She smiled firmly at Lark and asserted, "I love Jaris 'cause he's my friend, and, yeah, I had a little crush on him. But he's with Sereeta now, and I've gotten over any idea that we might date."

"You're really pretty, Alonee," Lark noted. "You should get a nice boyfriend. *I* think you're prettier than Sereeta."

Alonee grinned at her little sister. "I know one thing—I've got the best little sister in the world."

"You go out with Trevor sometimes, huh?" Lark asked.

"Yeah, he's my buddy too. That's all it is," Alonee replied. For a long time Alonee had kept it a secret that she was as crazy about Jaris as he was about Sereeta. Sometimes Jaris had a look on his face as if he suspected how she felt, but neither of them said anything. Alonee wanted it that way. Once Jaris knew she loved him in *that* way, their friendship would be ruined. Besides, Alonee cared about Sereeta too. They had also been friends all their lives. Alonee didn't begrudge Jaris and Sereeta their obvious happiness together.

"*I've* got a boyfriend," Lark suddenly confided. "His name is LeBron Mason, and he's a terrific baseball player. *All* the girls think he's awesome."

"Does he like you?" Alonee asked, smiling.

"He told me he hated me," Lark admitted. "but I don't believe that. My friend Jacklyn—she's older than me and she knows everything, especially about boys. She told me that LeBron must like me or he wouldn't have told me that he hated me."

"Sounds like Jacklyn knows her business," Alonee said.

"Yeah," Lark explained, "she says in the beginning a boy sorta hates the girl he likes 'cause he's mad at her for making him like her when he doesn't want to bother with girls. But deep down, he likes the girl and sometime he'll admit it. But it takes time. That's what Jacklyn said."

In the morning, Alonee printed out her science report for Mr. Buckingham. She had written it about the Hubble Space Telescope that was launched way back in 1990. Because it orbits outside Earth's atmosphere, it can take much better pictures of space. Over the years, astronauts from the United States, Russia, and other nations went into space to do repairs and upkeep on Hubble. Alonee had done a lot of research on the Internet and in the library. She had completed her report last night.

As the sheets came out of the printer, Alonee thought how she liked both her science teachers, Mr. Buckingham and Meredith Sanders. Mr. Buckingham was a very hard grader, but Alonee was a good student, so she didn't mind. Ms. Sanders was more generous in her grading, and most of the students liked her better.

Alonee tucked her science report into her backpack and started walking to school, as she did most mornings. When it was raining, one of her parents drove her. Usually Alonee walked with Sami Archer who left her home at about the same time.

"Hey Alonee!" Sami shouted from behind. She ran to catch up.

"I just finished my report for science this morning," Alonee said. "It was really interesting."

"I finished mine too," Sami replied, "but Buckingham gonna pick it to pieces most likely. He always finds somethin' wrong."

As they neared Tubman High, Sami remarked, "Look at herself standin' there in front of the school."

Alonee looked up at the impressive statue of Harriet Tubman with a serene look on her handsome face. Sami continued,

"Lissen up, girl. That lady there, she never went to school. She wouldn't know a microbe from a centipede. She saved folks from slavery. She helped the poor. She died in poverty. Been way over a hundred years now since her time and look, a school named for her right here. There she stands. She on postage stamps, and they even named a ship for her in World War II. She famous all over the world, and she never done a science report or a math test. Girl, we are knockin' ourselves out every day in high school, then there'll be college. And in a hundred years you think anybody is gonna know our names or put us on postage stamps?"

Alonee giggled. "You're right, Sami!"

Just then an old BMW pulled up in front of the school. A tall young man got out on the passenger side. He waved to the driver of the car, a gray-haired man, and then walked toward Tubman High.

"Whoah, look at that boy!" Sami exclaimed. "His grandpa delivers him in a BMW. An old one, but still a BMW."

"He's nice looking, from a distance anyway," Alonee noted. "He's tall, and I can see him smiling from way over here."

The young man seemed to be heading toward the science building, where Alonee was going. As she drew closer to him, she saw that he was even better looking than he had looked from a distance. He had light brown skin and close-cropped black hair. His features were classic.

The young man went into Mr. Buckingham's class and took a seat. Alonee was sitting right behind him.

"Oooooo," Ryann Kern cooed to her friend, Leticia Hicks, "isn't he gorgeous?"

Ryann and Leticia came from a small town in Alabama. Their families were close, and they had moved together to start an upholstery business. Ryann and Leticia were inseparable. They weren't yet comfortable in a large city, and they clung to each other. Now Leticia looked unhappy that Ryann was admiring the new boy. "Maybe," Alonee thought, "Leticia's worried that

9

Ryann is getting interested in boys. Maybe Leticia thinks she's going to lose the only friend she has around here."

Mr. Buckingham devoted the class to a discussion of space exploration. Just before the bell rang, he asked the students to turn in their reports. As Alonee lay her report on the teacher's desk, she found herself standing beside the young man who had sat in front of her. He was getting information on how he could catch up in class. Because he was coming into the class late in the year, he and his teachers had to work out a plan to get him up-to-date with the work. He looked at Alonee's report and then at Alonee. He smiled.

After class, as they were filing out of the classroom, the young man turned to Alonee. "I couldn't help but notice you did your report on the Hubble Space Telescope," he noted, then introduced himself. "Oh, I'm Oliver Randall. My father teaches astronomy at City College. He's a big fan of that telescope. I mean, when those astronauts went up to repair it last time during those space walks, my dad was so nervous he could hardly sleep."

"Yeah," Alonee replied. "That was exciting how they were out there in space fixing those delicate pieces of equipment. I'm Alonee Lennox. I love the pictures Hubble has sent. I think the first time I was really amazed was when it photographed a storm on Saturn."

"Man," Oliver remarked, "what a wild coincidence that the first student I talk to here at school just finished a report on my dad's favorite telescope!" He smiled. He had a wonderful, warm, bright smile.

"Where're you from, Oliver?" Alonee asked.

"Los Angeles," he responded. "I'm staying with my dad. He lives near here."

"Well, you'll like Tubman. It's a good school. The kids are friendly," Alonee told him.

"I can see that already," Oliver agreed. "Maybe we'll run into each other again

THE QUALITY OF MERCY

later on." He seemed to be hoping for that.

Later that day, Alonee noticed that Oliver was in an animated conversation with Jaris and Derrick. He seemed to be fitting right in. He had such a good personality that Alonee thought he'd know most of the junior class before long.

Alonee noticed something else too. Ryann was really taken by Oliver. She was trying desperately to find an opportunity to talk to him. It came when Oliver was standing near the English department looking at his class schedule.

"Hi," Ryann greeted him, "are you having trouble finding your next class?"

"Well," Oliver replied, "I'm supposed to be in a Mr. Pippin's class, and it should be around here."

"It's right around the corner. I'm going there too," Ryann said. "I'm Ryann Kern. Mr. Pippin isn't a very good teacher but he's okay. He's really old. That's why he can't teach very good."

"Well, sometimes older teachers have a lot to give too," Oliver objected.

"Yes, I suppose so," Ryann responded quickly, not wanting to say anything to offend this handsome young man. Back in Alabama she had a couple boyfriends, but nobody special. Ryann and Leticia would spend their time at parties standing together watching other kids dancing. This didn't seem to bother Leticia as much as it did Ryann.

"Do you like Tubman so far?" Ryann asked Oliver as they walked down the hallway. Ryann walked as slowly as possible, not wanting to get to Mr. Pippin's class any sooner than was necessary. She was hoping something would click between her and Oliver.

"Yeah, I like it," he replied. "I went to a much larger school in LA, and I like this better." When they walked into Mr. Pippin's class, Ryann waited until Oliver sat down, and she took the desk beside him. Mr. Pippin had no seating chart, and he didn't mind where people sat as long as they didn't visit with each other during class.

Ryann was starting to tell Oliver about Alabama, when Alonee came into the classroom. Mr. Pippin had not yet arrived and everybody was talking. To Ryann's frustration, Oliver looked at Alonee as she walked in and took a seat in front of them. He was staring at Alonee, and when she sat down he said, "Hi Alonee. We meet again." Ryann felt a rush of jealousy.

"Hi," Alonee replied, turning around and looking at Oliver. Alonee caught Ryann's angry glare, and she quickly faced the front of the class. "Poor Ryann," Alonee thought. "She's trying to make friends with Oliver, and he calls out a friendly greeting to me. Ryann shouldn't worry. I have no interest in Oliver Randall. He's a handsome, nice guy, but he's probably very boring. If he gets that excited about the Hubble telescope, how much fun can he be?" Alonee enjoyed science and all that, but Oliver didn't strike her as a boy she could grow to like. He wasn't like Jaris Spain.

As Alonee sat in English, she wondered if she would ever get over Jaris. She would have to. She couldn't go on comparing him to everybody she met. Jaris was permanently, hopelessly in love with Sereeta. Alonee had to accept that fact and forget about him. In her mind Alonee accepted that, but not yet in her heart. She wasn't totally comfortable with the idea that she would never be Jaris's girl.

Marko Lane leaned over toward the new student and asked, "Hey dude, what's your name?"

"Oliver Randall," Oliver replied.

"I'm Marko Lane. I'm pretty well connected around here. I'm the go-to-guy. If you can't figure something out, check with me."

"Thanks," was all Oliver said.

"Yeah," Marko went on, "like I'm here to tell you, in another couple minutes this Mr. Pippin'll come into this classroom.

Then for the next fifty minutes he's gonna waste our time like you wouldn't believe. I think he's got some dementia. He is *way* too old to be teaching. He needs to be off somewhere in one of those old folks homes."

"Give it a rest, Marko," Jaris said with disgust. "Let the new guy come to his own conclusions."

"How old is Mr. Pippin?" Oliver asked.

"Oh, he's gotta be getting close to sixty-five," Marko answered, "'cause he doesn't know where he's at half the time."

"My father is seventy, and he's still teaching astronomy at City College. He's brilliant. He lectures all over the country," Oliver said.

"Your *father* is seventy?" Marko gasped. "Dude, that's incredible."

Ryann noticed anger in Oliver's eyes. Clearly Marko had hurt his feelings. She wanted to do something to ingratiate herself to Oliver. "There's nothing wrong with old people teaching," Ryann stammered.

"I mean, it-it gives them something to do. It's better than them sitting in rocking chairs." Ryann expected Oliver to look at her gratefully, but instead he seemed to be looking at Alonee again.

Mr. Pippin arrived then, clutching his worn briefcase. He put the briefcase down on his desk and focused his gaze on Oliver Randall. "Good morning," he greeted the class. Then he continued, "I see we have our new student, Oliver Randall. I recognized the name, young man, because I attended UCLA a few years after your father graduated. As a postgraduate student, your father mentored me. We belonged to the same fraternity. And we had many enjoyable social times as fraternity brothers."

Oliver smiled and nodded. Then Mr. Pippin launched into a discussion of drama, choosing an act from Shakespeare's *Macbeth*. "Act IV is rich in interesting language," Mr. Pippin lectured. "Drama is often brought to life by striking imagery and language. Listen! 'Eye of newt and toe of frog, Wool of bat and tongue of dog, Adder's fork and blindworm's sting!'"

Marko raised his hand. "What's a blindworm?"

"A venomous lizard," Mr. Pippin explained. "The witches are mixing all of this into a powerful brew."

Marko leaned over to Derrick Shaw and whispered, "Oliver's mother must be old too. Maybe she's like the old witches!"

Derrick looked unhappy. He tried to ignore Marko. When Marko persisted, Derrick said, "Shhh!"

CHAPTER TWO

After class, Marko gathered a few students around him as Oliver remained in the classroom talking to Mr. Pippin. "How can that guy's father be seventy?" Marko protested. "He's like sixteen, right? I think something fishy's going on here."

Marko continued his speculation about Oliver Randall. "He's kinda strange looking. You guys notice that? His skin is way too smooth. Maybe he's some kind of an alien or something. Somebody from outer space?"

"You should know, Marko," Jaris Spain told him. "You gotta be from another planet, or maybe you jumped out of one of those black holes."

Alonee noticed Ryann hanging around the classroom, waiting for Oliver to get done talking with Mr. Pippin.

Finally Oliver came out and Ryann jumped into his path. "Hi Oliver," she beamed at him. "Get everything straightened out?"

"Yes, thanks," Oliver replied pleasantly, but he looked across the campus to where Alonee and some other girls stood. He hurried toward the little group. Ryann stood there clutching her books, her face dark with rage.

Sami was with Alonee as Oliver came walking up. "This is my friend, Sami Archer," Alonee made the introductions. "This is Oliver Randall, Sami."

"Hey dude, so your daddy teaches college, huh?" Sami remarked. "He must be one of those genius types."

Oliver grinned. "I don't' know about that," he answered, "but I'll tell you, when I saw Alonee's report was on the Hubble telescope, I bonded with the girl."

"That's cool," Sami said. "I sure do like looking up at the stars at night. My daddy showed me stuff like the Big Dipper, but most times I can't find it."

"Where do you guys eat lunch?" Oliver asked. "Do you buy something or bring your own stuff?"

"My mom usually packs my lunch," Alonee explained. "She makes good lunches, and it's healthier than the stuff you buy."

"Why don't you join us, dude," Sami offered. "We find a spot over there under the eucalyptus trees, and there's plenty room for everybody."

"Great," Oliver replied eagerly. "I brought my own lunch too."

"Your daddy pack your lunch?" Sami asked, giggling.

"I'm afraid not," Oliver said. "I pack my own. Like Alonee said, when you bring it from home it's healthier. Like I'll make a peanut butter sandwich on wheat and put carrot strips and cucumber slices on the top, and it's great."

The three of them found a spot under the trees and sat down on the grass. Alonee glanced across the campus and noticed Ryann still glaring in their direction. Alonee felt sorry for her. Again, Alonee thought if only Ryann knew—"I'm not trying to make a play for Oliver. He practically invited himself to join us for lunch, and it would've been unfriendly to snub him."

"So Oliver," Sami said, "how come you got that name? I don't run into a lot of Olivers around here."

Oliver laughed. "True. My father named me for Oliver Cromwell."

Alonee was amazed. Oliver Cromwell was an English Puritan leader who lived in the seventeenth century. Why would an African-American father name his child after an English leader who lived hundreds of years ago? "Oliver," she commented, "that's amazing. What made your dad name you for an English Puritan leader?"

Oliver laughed again. He almost choked on his peanut butter, carrot, and cucumber sandwich. He laughed easily and often. Alonee liked that about him. Jaris had an easy laugh too. That was one of his endearing qualities. But this guy was nothing like Jaris, Alonee thought. The things she loved about Jaris were too many and too complicated ever to find them in someone else. "Not *that* Oliver Cromwell," Oliver explained when he finally stopped laughing. "The other one."

"I hardly ever heard of the first Oliver Cromwell," Sami said. "You sayin' there's *another* dude with that name?"

"Yeah," Oliver replied. "His name was Oliver Cromwell, and he was born in New Jersey in 1753. He was a black farmer, and he joined up with General George Washington's army to drive out the British. When Washington crossed the Delaware in 1776, Oliver Cromwell was right there with him. And he fought in some other major battles during the Revolution too. He was a real American patriot, and he was black like us. So my father decided I ought to be named Oliver. He thought that would be a fine name for his first and only son, and Mom agreed."

"Wow!" Alonee exclaimed. "I thought I knew black history, but I never heard of this guy. We all hear about Crispus Attucks, the guy who died in the Boston Massacre, but Oliver Cromwell?"

Soon the trio was joined by Trevor, Derrick, Jaris, and Sereeta. Jaris and Sereeta sat close together. It used to bother Alonee to see how much Jaris loved another girl, but she didn't let it get to her anymore. They were happy together and that was that. Alonee refused to be selfish or mean-spirited enough to be offended by their happiness.

"You came to school this morning in a BMW," Sereeta said to Oliver. "I love those cars."

"My dad does too," Oliver responded. "He's always driven one. He gets them real used so they don't cost an arm and a leg. Mom likes Fords. She never drives anything but a Ford."

"So," Sami asked, "your parents live in different places, huh Oliver? What's that about? They divorced or something?" Sami didn't worry about asking personal questions. Alonee wouldn't do that.

"No," Oliver explained, "their lives just went in different directions. It's been that way for a long time. I spend half my time with Mom and half with Dad. It's Dad's turn now, or my turn to be with him."

"That can be hard," Sereeta commented. She had suffered very much after her parents' divorce when she was in middle school. She spent hours crying about it. When both her parents got into new relationships that seemed to exclude her, the pain got worse. Now she lived with her grandmother, and at last she had peace and stability.

"It hasn't been much of a hassle for me," Oliver responded. "Mom and Dad still care a lot about each other, and in the summer we're all together for vacations."

"Your mom got a career?" Sami asked.

"Yeah, she's an opera singer," Oliver said. "She's a soprano."

"You gotta be kiddin' me, dude!" Sami exclaimed. "Is that for real?"

Oliver smiled. "Yeah. She sings in little opera companies in the United States and Europe. She never got really famous, but she earns good money and loves it so much. She really likes to travel. Dad likes to hunker down in his little apartment and teach."

"That's quite a story," Alonee remarked.

"Yeah," Oliver went on, "Dad's been living around here for about ten years. He likes it here. It's a lot like South LA where he grew up. He likes to be close to his work, close to downtown. Mom is sometimes kind of, you know, horrified. She thinks inner city, and she thinks gangs, graffiti. She wasn't too cool about me going to Tubman High School. But I like it. I texted her the first day I got here. I told her I really felt at home. You guys are all so friendly. It's what I was hoping for."

"Well, you've joined the right gang, boy," Sami assured him. "We are the posse. These people you lookin' at right now. We been together a long time. We all look out for each other. So we got your back too, dude."

When they broke up after lunch, Alonee headed for biology. Meredith Sanders was a middle-aged teacher and taught biology with real enthusiasm.

"Hey Alonee Lennox," Ryann called out as Alonee passed.

"Hi Ryann," Alonee called back.

"Aren't you ashamed of yourself throwing yourself at that guy like you been doing?" Ryann said bitterly.

"What?" Alonee exclaimed.

"Don't play dumb with me," Ryann insisted. "You won't give him any peace. You're hanging onto him like sticky tape. He can't turn around without you there trying to grab onto him. What's *wrong* with you, girl? He can't even go to the john with you on his heels. You're making a fool of yourself."

Alonee sighed deeply. "Ryann, I'm sorry you're so upset," she said. "I'm not throwing myself at anybody. I wouldn't do that. Oliver is a nice guy, but I'm not the least bit interested in him, okay? Only reason we had lunch with him today is that he seemed lonely. We're being friendly to a new guy. We all were friendly to him, not just me. The bunch of us."

"You're not fooling me one little bit," Ryann persisted. "You've had your claws into him from the minute he stepped onto the campus. I see you flaunting yourself, Alonee Lennox. Well, all I can say is, he's a nice guy. Pretty soon he's gonna get sick and tired of a trashy girl like you dogging his steps!"

"I'm sorry you feel like that Ryann," Alonee sighed. Leticia was standing on the sidelines, staring at Ryann. As Alonee walked into biology, she heard Leticia yell at Ryann. "Girl, you are making such an idiot of yourself. Everybody was looking at you screaming like that!"

"I don't care," Ryann shouted back, tears in her voice. "I just hate that girl so much! I just hate that Alonee Lennox so much!"

Alonee was embarrassed for Ryann. It was bad enough earlier in the year when she pretended to have been robbed of a hundred dollars. She finally had to admit it didn't happen. Ryann had thrown the school into turmoil with her accusations. Now she was acting stupid again. Alonee thought maybe she was cracking up because she was so uncomfortable in the new city atmosphere after living so long in that small Alabama town.

After the last class, Alonee started walking home. Often she walked home with Sami, but today she walked alone. Then, after a few minutes, Jasmine fell in step beside her. "Hey Alonee, what do you think of the new dude?" Jasmine asked.

"He seems nice," Alonee answered.

"Marko thinks he's weird," Jasmine remarked. "I don't believe he's got a seventy-year-old daddy. He's lying. If some old dude was to come around asking me for a date I'd whack him in the head. The mother has got to be much younger. Marko thinks he's lying 'bout everything."

"Why would Marko think that?" Alonee asked. To herself she thought, "Could it be because Marko's an idiot?"

"The whole story sounds fake," Jasmine continued. "I mean, the old dad teaching astronomy, and then somebody says the mother's an opera singer or something. I bet Oliver made it all up. I bet he has some dark past that he's trying to cover up with a lot of wild stories. Y'hear what I'm saying?"

"He seems okay to me," was all Alonee said.

"You're too goody-two-shoes, Alonee. You're so gullible," Jasmine told her. "Oh, Oliver is good-looking. I'll give him that. He's the best looking dude I ever saw at Tubman. Marko is handsome, but he's better looking than Marko. 'Course I'd never tell Marko that."

"Well," Alonee replied, "I take people at their word until or unless they do something wrong."

"Marko thinks maybe he come here to start trouble," Jasmine suggested darkly.

"What kind of trouble would he want to start?" Alonee asked.

"I don't know," Jasmine asserted. "Marko's mother, she listens to this guy who's on the radio all night. He got stories about what happened in the 1950s in Roswell, New Mexico. Aliens landed and the government covered it up. They had all these little alien bodies, and they hid them so's not to scare people. Well, Marko's mom says this guy on the radio has all kinds of intelligent people come on. They say that aliens are landing all the time, and they're walking around with us. I don't know if that stuff is true or made up, but it might be true. Maybe this Oliver is one of them, you know?"

"Jasmine," Alonee sighed. "I hope you're joking . . . I really, *really* hope you're joking."

"Maybe, or maybe not," said Jasmine. "Marko's mother says millions of people listen to this radio show, and they believe it. Maybe there are aliens here, and they got a way of looking just like us."

"Well," Alonee responded, "let's just hope for the best." She thought to herself that Marko was acting even more stupidly than usual. Although Marko's mom was a businesswoman who ran a house cleaning service, she had some strange ideas. Science fiction was real to her.

When Alonee got home, Lark was in the living room doing her homework. She looked up at Alonee and announced, "He yanked my braids."

"Who did?" Alonee asked.

"LeBron Mason," Lark told her. "He sneaked up behind me and yanked on my braids. I think Jacklyn's right. I think he is really starting to like me, Alonee."

Alonee's other sister Jolene was already in the kitchen helping Mom start dinner. Four-year-old Tucker, the only boy in the family, was playing with the cat. Tucker was born when Alonee was twelve. She was really excited to welcome a new sibling, but she was amazed at how Dad reacted. He had been wanting a boy for so long that he went crazy. Dad loved his three girls with all his heart, but he wanted a boy. He had almost given up hope when Tucker was born. Finally Floyd Lennox had his son and he was overjoyed.

"Dawna," Dad had said to her mother at the time, "this completes our family. Our beautiful girls and now a boy. It's a blessing, Dawna."

Mom had laughed and said, "It works for me, Floyd."

Alonee loved Tucker even though she knew he was spoiled rotten. She even happily helped spoil him. He was ridiculously cute and lovable. No matter what mischief he got into, everybody was ready to forgive him. He would blink those big dark eyes with the long lashes and flash that dimpled smile—and all would be well.

"Hi Alonee," he greeted her from the floor, where he was playing.

"Hi Tucker. Was preschool fun today?" Alonee asked.

"No. Teacher made frying saucers," Tucker said.

"What are frying saucers?" Alonee asked.

Jolene laughed and explained. "Flying saucers. They saw a space movie, and they had these paper plates painted silver, with little space men coming off them."

Alonee recalled her walk home with Jasmine. "Marko Lane, that troublemaker at Tubman, he believes stuff like that. He thinks our new student, Oliver Randall, is an alien. Oliver is so handsome that the girls are freaking out over him. I guess Marko is jealous because the girls aren't paying as much attention to him now. It's kind of hilarious when you think about it."

"Do you like him, Alonee?" Lark asked, momentarily forgetting about LeBron pulling her braids.

"He's nice. He's interesting," Alonee responded. "I mean, what's not to like?"

"But you like Jaris better, huh?" Lark said.

"Sure," Alonee said. "I've known Jaris a long time. We're good friends. We got a lot of history together. I've just met Oliver."

Alonee knew Lark meant something else, but Alonee didn't want to go into it. A kind of fence surrounded Alonee's heart, a little garden that belonged to Jaris Spain. Alonee was unconsciously protecting that little garden from interlopers—like Oliver Randall—who might step on all her memories.

CHAPTER THREE

A little later and just before the family sat down to dinner, fire engine sirens suddenly wailed outside. Alonee's father was on duty at his station. Whenever they heard fire engines and he wasn't home, they were always concerned. But he was well trained and smart—an excellent firefighter—and they knew he was as safe as it was possible for him to be.

"Sounds close," Mom remarked. "I suppose your dad is on the engine going there . . ."

Mom was used to the idea that Dad fought fires. Last fall terrible brush fires had flamed up and threatened hundreds of homes. Floyd Lennox was one of the firefighters who had saved seven hundred homes. And, with his fellow firefighters, he grieved the loss of seventy homes. Mom knew her husband was good at his job, yet there was always that nagging worry. She never lost sight of the danger.

Lark yelled, "It's on TV right now . . . there's a fire at Tubman High School! Right now!"

Alonee looked at the screen. Black smoke was curling around the statue of Harriet Tubman.

Alonee's mother paused in her dinner-making chores to watch the televised news. "Looks like they're getting it beaten down," she noted. "Can't see any fire, just smoke. Those firefighters do such a great job. I'm so proud of your father and his buddies."

The news reporters said a fire had been started in a trash barrel behind the science building. The back wall of the building was scorched. There was a lot of smoke but no serious damage. School would be held as usual the next day.

"Those fools who like to start fires for some excitement," Mom grumbled. "Probably kids fooling around in the evening without any parental supervision. That's why your father, and I decided that I'd be a stay-at-home mom. Can't let kids run wild on their own."

"Arson is really a terrible crime," Alonee remarked. "You never know what's going to happen. You could start out doing a prank and end up hurting or killing someone."

"I bet Daddy was right there putting out that fire," Jolene declared proudly. She was always bragging about her father in her fourth-grade classroom. "Some kids brag about how much money their dads make. But I always say my daddy is a firefighter and saves people and their houses."

"That's right, baby," Mom affirmed.

When Floyd Lennox came home, he talked about the fire at the school. "They're doing an investigation of the fire to find out what happened. Right now it looks like somebody just tossed a burning cigarette or something into the trash barrel. Could've been done on purpose, using a match or some incendiary."

"Maybe somebody didn't like the grade they got in science," Alonee suggested. Mr. Buckingham was the hardest grader at the school, and some tests had just been returned.

At school the next day, you couldn't even see where the fire had been. The wall was whitewashed, and it looked perfect. The old trash can was gone, replaced by a new one. Most of the students didn't even know what had happened but a few did.

"I figure somebody's got it in for Mr. Buckingham," Trevor Jenkins commented to Alonee. "The fire started right in back of his classroom. He failed a couple guys yesterday, and one of them was swearing a blue streak."

"Who was that?" a boy asked.

"Eric Carney," Trevor answered. "I don't know the guy but he was spoutin' fire."

Alonee didn't know Eric well either. Nobody really did. He was a scruffy kid who always wore ill fitting clothes. He had a bad attitude. He seemed angry most of the time. But Alonee didn't know if he was angry enough to start a fire in a trash can to make a point.

Marko Lane had his own theory. "Mighty funny," he opined, "that the first day that new guy comes on campus with all his weird stories, something like this happens. You guys ever see that old horror movie about the girl who could start fires just by looking at people?"

"Don't be silly, Marko," Alonee protested. "Oliver likes Mr. Buckingham's class. He was all excited about it."

Leticia Hicks and Ryann Kern had just gotten off the school bus. They were talking about the fire too. "Remember when we had those fires at our school in Alabama?" Ryann asked. "They never figured out who did it. They were a bunch of little fires, but it was scary."

"Yeah," Leticia recalled, "I remember thinking some pyromaniac was loose. We were all nervous."

"Look! Over there!" Ryann gasped. "Isn't that Oliver getting out of the BMW?"

"Oh please," Leticia said, "you're not gonna get all goony again over him are you? He doesn't even know you're alive."

Leticia was a tall, plain girl. Her eyes were a bit too close together, and her face was squarish, made worse by a bad hairstyle. Short-clipped hair hung on both sides of her face. She always had a dour expression on her face, as if she were disappointed about something.

"How about the fire?" Jasmine asked as she walked up the group. "Something going wrong around here. Don't forget I told you first."

"Yeah," Leticia agreed, "I got bad feelings about that new guy too. It's like something evil has come to Tubman High. Remember that Macbeth thing we did yesterday?"

Jasmine nodded, "Yeah. 'Something wicked this way comes.' Right? Isn't that the truth? You hear what I'm saying?"

"Right!" Leticia answered, her face brightening. A brief bond had formed between the two girls, Jasmine and Leticia. It was an unlikely bond between the beautiful Jasmine, who had her pick of boys, and Leticia, who had long ago given up hope of attracting a boyfriend.

"Look, here he comes," Jasmine whispered.

"It's spooky," Leticia whispered back, "that old man in the BMW delivering him to school. He said it's his father, but I bet it's not really his father. Why would such an old man have a son sixteen years old?"

"You guys," Alonee declared, "you're letting your wild imaginations run away with you. Oliver has nothing to do with the fire in the trash can. Some stupid vandals started it for some excitement. Don't make a big thing out of it."

For the moment, Ryann sided with Alonee. "Why're you guys picking on Oliver?" she demanded. "I like him. I think he's really nice." Ryann then stomped off in a huff. Leticia looked after her, sadness on her face. She was losing her friend, her *only* friend.

"You see?" Leticia said bitterly to Jasmine. "We've been friends all our lives back in Alabama. We were on each other's side no matter what. Now she's gone nuts over some creepy guy, and that's all she thinks about. She won't even go to the mall with me anymore. So much for loyalty!"

Jasmine nodded. "Girls are sometimes like that. I guess most times they are. If they got to decide between a girlfriend and a new boyfriend, the girl gets tossed real fast, just like a wad of chewed-up gum!"

Alonee was glad to go to American history and forget about all the dramatic talk swirling around Oliver Randall.

Ms. McDowell was talking about terrorism and what a threat it posed to the world. "It's rooted in hatred and suspicion. People don't know each other, and they don't trust each other. We look at people we don't know through stereotypes. It's easy to hate people because they are darker or lighter than us, because they don't speak the same language we do, because they belong to a different religion, because they wear strange clothes, or because they are poor."

Oliver Randall was not in this class, but another student, Carissa Polson, referred to him. She wore her hair in cornrows, and she was a very pretty girl. She dated Kevin Walker, who had come to Tubman from Texas only a little while ago. She raised her hand and added a comment. "This new student we have, he's just been here a day and a half, and I've heard kids whispering about him. He's a little different. He's new and we don't know him yet. So they're making up crazy stories about him"

"Exactly what I'm saying, Carissa," Ms. McDowell replied. "When we don't know someone, we fill in the blanks, often with our worst fears."

Marko Lane raised his hand. "Yeah," he objected, "but what if somebody comes along and they really are bad. And you figure you gotta stop them before they do something?"

"Marko," Ms. McDowell said, "we have to have good, sound reasons to reach a conclusion that someone is a danger. If you have such reasons, then, of course, you must take action. But you can't base your negative ideas about a stranger on the mere fact that he is different from the rest of us."

"Isn't it better," Marko insisted, "to come down on somebody who looks like he's out to make trouble, even if it turns out you're wrong? I mean, isn't that better than being a wishy-washy person who thinks everybody is nice. Like, what I'm saying is, if you crack down on the wrong person, well, too bad. But if you let a really bad dude fall through the cracks, and he ends up hurting a lot of people, that's worse isn't it?"

"In other words, Marko," Ms. McDowell reasoned, "punish a whole lot of innocent people rather than let some guilty person free to do harm."

"Well, yeah," Marko agreed. "I guess that's what I think."

Derrick Shaw raised his hand. He usually didn't have anything insightful to say, but Ms. McDowell listened to him as intently as she did to any other student. "What Marko says," Derrick started to say, "I mean, it sounds right. But what if I'm the innocent dude who gets hammered? What if I'm the one gets busted when I didn't do anything? I don't want to be the poor joker who didn't do anything wrong and ends up lynched."

"Ah," Ms. McDowell exclaimed, smiling. "There's the rub, isn't it? It's OK to have other innocent people dragged in just to catch the guilty one, but it better not be me."

At lunchtime, Alonee wasn't sure how she felt about Oliver Randall joining the

posse. Part of her hoped he'd go somewhere else so that they could just be
together as usual. Part of her felt sorry for
him and didn't want him to feel excluded.
But the decision wasn't up to Alonee. As
she headed into their favorite spot under the
eucalyptus trees, Oliver was already looking right at home with Jaris, Derrick,
Destini, Sami, and Sereeta. Oliver turned
and gave her a special smile.

"My grandmother likes opera, Oliver,"
Sereeta was saying. "She'd probably enjoy
hearing your mom sing. I've got the most
amazing grandma. She likes all kinds of
music, even rap. Sometimes I'll have this
blasting music on, and she's snapping her
fingers like she's a kid." Sereeta opened her
yogurt cup and asked, "What operas has
your mom done?"

Alonee got a little nervous. Unlike
Marko and Jasmine, she didn't believe that
Oliver was lying about his background. She
did think maybe he was embellishing it a
bit to make himself more interesting. If he

47

had invented the opera-singing mom to make himself more colorful. Then he would probably know nothing about opera, and he'd be embarrassed in front of everybody. Alonee didn't want that to happen. Something deep inside her wanted him to be real. She wasn't sure why she felt that way, but he stirred that kind of feeling in her. And she knew she would be genuinely sad if he turned out to be a liar.

"Let's see," Oliver said thoughtfully. "I've seen her in some. She was Marguerite in *Faust*. I was pretty young when I saw that, and it was scary. The stage settings were very dark and spooky, and it was strange to see my mom all made up. But I think the opera I remember most was when she played Madame Butterfly. Wow, a beautiful black lady as the little Japanese girl who got left behind. I saw her at lunch making spaghetti, and at night she was Butterfly. Wow!"

"That must have been exciting for you," Jaris suggested.

"Yeah, it was," Oliver said. "But selfish kid that I was, I would of rather had her home."

"How about you, Oliver?" Derrick asked. "Do you sing too? You want to get into show business?"

Oliver laughed. "No, I sing a little just for fun. But I'm no opera singer."

"Maybe you'll be an astronomer like your dad," Alonee commented.

Oliver shrugged. He looked right at Alonee and starting talking. "You know. Alonee, when I first met you and saw that you did that report on the Hubble telescope—you know what really blew my mind? The thing that really made my parents decide to live apart for much of the year was that telescope. I remember Dad wasn't coming home, and Mom was getting really upset, and she goes, 'Louis, something's come between us. Something big. I don't know what it is but. . . .' And then Dad says, 'Katrina, I swear there is no other woman. There never could be.' 'So then why do you go away for weeks and months and not seem to notice if I am home or not?' Mom says. And then he explains that he's doing all this work on the Hubble telescope, symposiums, papers, research. They decided then that he would spend his time with Hubble, and she would go full-time on opera, and in the summers we'd be a family again."

"Wow, I'd hate it if my folks lived like that," Derrick remarked.

"Me too," Jaris agreed. "One time I thought maybe they were having trouble, and I freaked."

Oliver looked thoughtful for a moment, then he said, "I guess what makes it okay is that they still love each other. When we get together on vacations, we have a ball. Weird, huh? I bet you never met somebody like me."

"I hate to tell you this, child," Sami started to say, finishing her sandwich, "but Marko Lane has this theory about you." A smile tugged at Sami's lips as she spoke.

"Oh yeah, I've met him," Oliver responded. "He's an interesting character. He wants to send Mr. Pippin off to the rest home."

"Well, Marko," Sami continued, "he thinks maybe you're from outer space, boy. He thinks your skin is way too smooth. He thinks your story is too strange to be true. Marko's mom, she listens to this radio program about space folks dropping in on us from time to time and sort of infiltratin' our world. So Marko, he figures maybe you just jumped off a UFO or somethin'."

"He's joking, right?" Oliver asked.

Sami made a helpless gesture. "You never know with that dude. He got to find somethin' wrong with everybody. Make him feel good, I guess."

"Well," Oliver told them all, "if he brings that up again, just tell him that I came in peace."

They all let out such a roar of laughter, that they almost shook some of the leaves off the eucalyptus trees. Alonee thought as

51

she was laughing that—yes—Oliver *did* belong in the posse. She was glad he'd come today. He would always be welcome.

Later that day, as Alonee was starting her walk home after classes, she noticed Oliver coming toward her. His father hadn't come to pick him up yet. "Hi Alonee," he called.

"Hi," Alonee called back, noticing again how handsome he was, how perfect his features, how endearing his smile.

"Alonee, I don't want to get personal," Oliver started, "but . . . I was, uh . . . just wondering if you had a boyfriend. I mean, you're such a pretty girl, and you got such a nice personality. You probably have a boyfriend. I've got no business prying into your personal life anyway, but . . ." His voice trailed off.

"No, I don't have a boyfriend," Alonee stated. To herself she said, "I do have a boyfriend—his name is Jaris, but only in my dreams. Some little girls have imaginary friends, and I've always had an imaginary boyfriend."

Out loud, she did say, "But thanks for those nice compliments."

"Oh, you're welcome," he replied. A look of excitement came to his face. "Well then, maybe it would be okay if sometime I asked you out? I mean, I know we don't know each other well. But just for a movie or something, you know. . . . If you wouldn't feel comfortable going out with me right away, I could wait until we knew each other better. Then we could maybe . . . you know, go for pizza or something."

Alonee wasn't quite sure what came over her. She had made up her mind right from the beginning that, no matter how attractive Oliver Randall was, she really wasn't interested in him. She tried to convince herself that it wasn't only because he wasn't Jaris. Surely she was beyond that. She had turned down many boys because they weren't Jaris. She felt like a fool, and yet she turned them down again and again. Now, suddenly, she thought, "Well, even though he isn't Jaris, maybe it would be fun to go somewhere with him." So Alonee smiled and said, "I think we know each other well enough for pizza, Oliver. I'd enjoy going out with you."

"Yeah?" he said, a big grin on his face. He looked like a little boy who just found out he was getting what he wanted for Christmas. "So," he went on, "this Sunday, down at the pier, there's a little garage band playing. I know the guys. They got a good sound. So maybe we could go down there and then get some fish fry?"

"Yeah," Alonee said, "that sounds nice."

It was not that Alonee hadn't gone out with boys in the past year. Ever since she was fifteen, she went on group dates. When she turned sixteen, she went out with Trevor Jenkins and other boys.

But these boys were not Jaris, and eventually they just went back to being friends.

"Great," Oliver exclaimed. "I'll be at your house around eleven on Sunday morning."

"I'll be waiting," Alonee said.

"Hey," Oliver noted, "here comes my dad. Want a ride home? Then I could see where you live too."

"Okay," Alonee agreed. She felt funny. The afternoon blue sky had turned a cartoonish blue—bluer than blue.

Mr. Randall looked every bit his seventy years, but he was an elegant looking man. His skin was very dark, and his hair was salt and pepper.

"Dad," Oliver said to him, "this is Alonee Lennox, the girl I was telling you about. Alonee, this is my dad."

"Hello Alonee," Mr. Randall said. "My son can't stop talking about you."

"Thank you," Alonee replied. Alonee felt as if she were riding in Cinderella's coach. She felt strange and excited, and she didn't think of Jaris Spain at all during the ride home as she gave Mr. Randall directions.

"There," Alonee said when they approached her house. "The house with the rose bushes in front. Mom planted them a long time ago. She loves roses. That's where I live."

Mr. Randall pulled into the driveway, and Alonee got out and thanked him for the ride. Then she hurried into her house and sat down on the couch to catch her breath. She felt as if she had been running, and she couldn't breathe for a few minutes. It was a strange sensation.

CHAPTER FOUR

The next day, when Alonee sat down in Mr. Buckingham's class, Oliver looked for her. When he saw her, he came over to sit beside her. Derrick Shaw usually sat in that spot, and he came as usual and stood there.

"Oh man, did I take your place?" Oliver asked.

"Yeah," Derrick said with a smile, "but it's okay." Derrick walked over and sat someplace else.

"Mr. Buckingham doesn't care where we sit," Alonee told Oliver. "Just so we don't talk during class. He'll bust you for that." Once Alonee—she remembered—made the mistake of making a comment to a classmate, and Mr. Buckingham came down on her fast and hard. Alonee was a good student, and Mr. Buckingham liked good students, but in general he didn't like any students too much. He was too into his subject matter and his agenda—saving the environment—to be involved with his students.

Mr. Buckingham was a tall, dark man whose ancestry included a line of African kings, he claimed. Everybody agreed that he was an excellent, brilliant teacher but that he graded without mercy. He often said that anyone who missed a major test could have only one acceptable excuse: a death notice.

Mr. Buckingham came into class this morning in an exceptionally bad mood. "Before we begin class," he announced, "I want anyone to tell me what the figure of a duck on the curb near the storm sewer means to you."

Derrick raised his hand. "I guess some kid was like painting graffiti?" he offered.

"No!" Mr. Buckingham roared with such force that Derrick leaned back in his chair and looked terrorized. "Has anyone else an explanation to offer?" the teacher demanded.

Oliver put his hand in the air: "It's a symbol to remind us that ducks and other wildlife need a clean waterway to survive and that, if you dump pollutants in the storm drain, you harm them."

"Yeah," Alonee added, "because what we dump down the drainpipes in our houses goes through the sewer treatment plant and is processed, but what goes into the storm drain goes right to the ocean."

"Exactly!" Mr. Buckingham said, calming down. "How many of you hose down your driveways?"

A few hands went up.

"You must never, *ever* do that!" Mr. Buckingham cried. "Sweep the driveway with a broom. When you hose it down, you're washing oil and other contaminants down the storm drain. Don't overwater your lawns because then the fertilized overflow goes into the storm drains as well."

Mr. Buckingham leaned on his podium, a kind of cold smile on his face. "I have a true story to share with you, people. In my neighborhood, there is a man with no respect for the environment. I saw him dumping oil, paint thinner, and other poisons into the storm drain. I warned him that if I ever saw him doing that again, he was in trouble. He cursed me. Well, when he did it again, I called the police."

Mr. Buckingham's smile spread into a kind of leer. "The police sent investigators and a hazmat team," Mr. Buckingham announced. "'Hazmat' is short for 'hazardous materials.' They made quite a show in all their protective gear. My criminal neighbor was outraged, but I stood up for the environment and was proud to do so. I want you people to do likewise. Be aware of anyone pouring filth into the storm drains. Report them! Show them no mercy. They have no mercy on the land or its inhabitants, both animal and human."

Marko Lane exchanged looks with Trevor Jenkins. Both were thinking the same thing. It took a lot of nerve to do what Mr. Buckingham had done.

"We're turning our waterways into poisonous pits," Mr. Buckingham raved on. "I shall not stand by without doing my duty, and neither should you. Remember, people, you are young. Your lives are before you. You will suffer more from this abuse of the earth than older people like me. Have a care for your children!"

After the class, everyone was talking about Mr. Buckingham's rant. "He's over the top," Marko exclaimed. "I mean, who wants a dirty lake, but, man, he's talking war with the people around us!"

"Maybe," Alonee responded, "but what he says is true."

"I think he's great," Oliver chimed in. "How many people have that kind of passion for *anything*? Sometimes I think we're all like sheep, quietly marching to our doom. I wasn't raised that way. My father has been an activist for a lot of causes. He marched in the civil rights demonstrations. He was water-hosed as a kid during one of the marches."

"Yeah, well," Marko countered, "if the guy next door is pouring a little paint down the storm drain, I'm not calling the police. I mean, stuff just happens . . ."

"Did you notice Eric Carney glaring at Mr. Buckingham all during class?" Alonee asked Oliver. "He's the guy who sits in the last row, and he's always got car magazines tucked into his textbook, which he reads during class. Then he does badly in the tests."

"You think he might've set that trash can on fire behind Mr. Buckingham's classroom?" Oliver asked.

"Well," Alonee said. "I guess it's wrong to point the finger at anybody without any proof. It could have been just somebody tossing a cigarette butt. It might have smoldered and then suddenly started burning."

"You have a sensitive conscience," Oliver observed. "I like that."

Alonee smiled. "Don't you?" she asked.

"Mostly," Oliver replied. "On my planet we have a strong sense of right and wrong."

Alonee gave Oliver a playful shove. "Oh you!" she laughed.

"Alonee," Oliver told her, "you'll like that band on Sunday. I knew the guys in Los Angeles, and they've come here to do a few gigs. They haven't gotten any big breaks yet, like a record deal, but they are so good. They play loud, edgy music that gets under your skin. One guy plays the guitar, and the other one plays the drums. And their lyrics are fly."

Alonee smiled at Oliver. His eyes were amazing. They were the color of sparkling root beer. "I'm looking forward to it," Alonee said.

On Sunday Oliver showed up at Alonee's house in his father's BMW. "Dad says if I don't' bring this baby back in the same condition I took it in, he's going to send me to the moon," Oliver said.

When they arrived at the beach, there was a festival atmosphere with games for kids and craft booths. Oliver reached out and took Alonee's hand. His grasp was very gentle. "See over there," he pointed, "where the pier starts? The guys are setting up right now."

"Are those your friends?" Alonee asked, seeing a white guy with red hair and a red soul patch, and a bald black guy with earrings and a nose ring.

"Yeah," Oliver said. "The name of the band is Life of Amphibians. Todd's the redhead and Rex is the baldy. He shaves it clean."

They walked over to where the band was setting up. Oliver introduced Alonee to his friends, and Todd added, "We're doing a little open mike in a while. You like to sing?"

"No way," Alonee protested. "I sing a little in church, in the praise choir, but the good singers thankfully drown me out."

"I bet you have a nice voice," Oliver suggested. "Your speaking voice is so nice. You gotta have a nice singing voice."

"Forget it, Oliver," Alonee said. "Do you want me to embarrass you?"

Todd looked at Alonee and said, "You'd sure look pretty singing up there. Everybody's making so much noise it wouldn't matter if you forgot the words or something. Me and Rex'll just play louder,"

Alonee looked at Oliver, who egged her on. "Go do it."

"Only on one condition," Alonee insisted, "that you go on after me, Oliver."

"Alonee, I don't sound too good," Oliver said.

"If I'm going to make a fool of myself, then you are too," Alonee demanded.

Oliver grinned, "You're on, babe," he agreed.

Alonee didn't want to go up on the stage, but the idea was exciting. She wasn't used to doing crazy things like this. It was kind of fun to be breaking out of her safe zone. Sometimes she thought she played things too safe.

"What are you singing?" Rex asked.

Alonee sang an old song that was a favorite of her father, "Sweet Child O' Mine," and, though she started out a little wobbly, she soon hit her stride. The band backed her up so well that she almost sounded good. A little crowd had gathered and at the end of her song, they gave Alonee a nice round of applause and a few whistles.

Alonee gave Oliver a gentle shove and said, "Okay, your turn."

Oliver went up on the stage and yelled to his buddies, "Okay Rex, Todd, hang onto your guitars and drums. This boy needs help, if you know what I'm sayin'!"

Oliver sang Otis Redding's "(Sittin' on) The Dock of the Bay."

Alonee was stunned by the power of his voice. He had a wonderful rolling baritone. As the words swept over the crowd, people abandoned their games and craft booths and gathered to listen. Oliver delivered "Look like nothing's gonna change / Everything still remains the same" with a powerful weariness. By the time he finished the last line, about a hundred people were cheering and stamping their feet.

The older folks loved the song and the younger ones were enchanted by the handsome young man with the big voice. Oliver jumped off the makeshift stage and grabbed Alonee's hand. "Let's eat!" he declared. "We can still hear them from the fish fry place."

"Oliver," Alonee said, "you're good!"

"So were you," Oliver replied. "I'm hungry."

"I had no idea you had such a good voice," Alonee remarked as they headed for the restaurant.

"Those guys in the band helped me a lot," Oliver said.

"You would have sounded great without a band," Alonee said.

As they sat eating fish fry, Alonee made a suggestion. "We have a junior-senior talent show coming up in a few weeks. It's always so lame for the Tubman juniors. If you entered, we'd have an exciting performer.

Usually we get these lame magic tricks and comedy routines that aren't funny. I bet you'd be the star of the show, Oliver."

"I don't think so," Oliver objected.

"Please," Alonee begged. "It would be so exciting to have a junior who could actually sing."

"Well," Oliver said, "maybe."

"Mr. Wingate is the head of the fine arts and drama department," Alonee persisted, "and he's signing up students. The deadline is next Wednesday, but you could sign up today."

"On a Sunday?" Oliver asked.

"Mr. Wingate has signup sheets in a box outside the door of the drama building. Anyone who wants to can go by there and put their name and phone number down. Then they just stick it back in the box," Alonee explained.

"Well okay," Oliver agreed. "For you, Alonee."

After they finished eating, they drove by Tubman High School and parked in the empty parking lot. Alonee and Oliver walked to the drama building and found the signup sheets. "Let's see," Oliver said. "Name, phone number, and talent—I should say 'singer,' right?"

"Right," Alonee giggled. "If any more comedians and magicians show up, I think poor Mr. Wingate is going to cancel the whole show."

Just then Alonee noticed something unusual across the lawn, behind the science building. Right behind Mr. Buckingham's classroom, someone seemed to be at the door. A head was bobbing.

"Oliver," Alonee said, "I wonder if someone is over by the science building doing maintenance or something. I think I saw a person behind Mr. Buckingham's classroom."

A chill ran through Alonee's body. Something was wrong. When she looked in that direction, whoever was over there seemed to duck out of sight, as if he or she knew she had seen them.

"I don't think they do repairs on a Sunday except if there's an emergency," Oliver replied.

"Oliver, I don't feel good about this," Alonee said. "I think something's wrong."

"I'll go over and take a look," Oliver said, as he started over.

As he walked toward the science building, Alonee hurried to match his long stride. He stopped and took a firm hold of her arm. "No Alonee, you stay here," he commanded. "I don't know what's going on over there. I don't want you going with me. Just stay here. If something's really wrong, I'll yell, and you call for help on your cell phone, okay?"

"I don't want you walking into something dangerous either, Oliver," Alonee objected, "Maybe we should just call nine-one-one now and let them handle it."

"No, it might just be kids who're using the parking lot to go skateboarding or something," Oliver speculated. "I don't want to call out the infantry unless it's necessary." He smiled at her and put his hand on her shoulder. "Stay here, Alonee, and I'll go see."

Alonee was surprised how concerned she was for his safety. He had gotten to her in the past few days. Even though she told herself she wasn't going to get involved with anyone, she was deeply worried when she saw him going around the corner of the science building. Alonee took out her cell phone. Her hands were trembling.

Alonee heard Oliver yell, "Hey you!"

She wanted to call 9-1-1 right then and there, but she hesitated. What if they were only kids, as he thought?

But Alonee couldn't just stand and wait as he told her to. She ran toward the science building, clutching her cell phone. She heard sounds of a struggle—grunts and gasps.

When Alonee reached the patch of grass behind Mr. Buckingham's classroom, she was shocked to see Oliver grappling with a guy just a little less than his size. The guy had already landed a punch to Oliver's face. Oliver's right eyebrow was bloody, and a trickle of red ran down his temple.

Then Alonee recognized the other guy—Eric Carney. Oliver was getting the better of the fight now. He had Eric pinned down. Oliver wrenched Eric's right arm behind his back and said to the struggling boy beneath him, "Take it easy, dude. Just relax. Don't make this any worse on yourself."

"Don't bust my arm, man," Eric cried. "I wasn't doin' anything. When I saw you I just got scared and ran. I wasn't doin' anything man."

"Bro, you think you can behave yourself if I let you up?" Oliver asked.

"Yeah, yeah," Eric said. When Oliver got up and freed him, he staggered to his feet. He saw the blood on Oliver's face and apologized. "Hey man, I'm sorry. I didn't mean to hit you. I just turned and saw this big guy comin' after me and I just freaked. I'm sorry."

"So," Oliver said to the trembling young man, "what were you doing here on a Sunday afternoon at the back door of Mr. Buckingham's classroom? I'm sure you've got a really good explanation."

"Should I call the police?" Alonee asked.

"No, no, please don't do that," Eric pleaded. "Please, my dad'll kill me if I get in trouble like that. He'll kill me. I was just . . . I mean . . . I thought I could get in. I can sometimes get in places that are locked with my tools . . ."

Oliver nodded. "You're telling me that you're a burglar?"

"No, I'm not. I'm not. But there's another test in science next week, and Buckingham keeps the tests in the top drawer of his desk. I thought maybe, you know. I flunked the test last week, and I thought I could find copies of the test and . . ." Eric's voice trailed off.

"And cheat." Oliver finished his sentence.

"Yeah, man," Eric whined, "Like my old man, he'll whip me with a strap if I get an F in science. Maybe you don't believe me." Eric pulled up his T-shirt. Both Oliver and Alonee saw red marks where a whip had recently struck.

Oliver exchanged a look with Alonee.

"That's wrong, man," Oliver declared. "Your father shouldn't be doing that. You should get help."

"We got six kids in our family," Eric explained. "You hear what I'm sayin'? My old man works hard, and he keeps us fed and clothed. He's good to my mom. If the social services came around, they'd bust up my family. We'd end up in foster care or a group home. Mom couldn't handle that. Listen man, I can manage. It's okay. Just don't call the cops on me, okay?"

Alonee could hear Oliver's deep sigh from a few feet away.

"Buckingham, he's an old devil," Eric continued. "He likes to flunk kids. All he cares about are those dumb animals he's trying to save. He doesn't care about us. I was having trouble in Ms. McDowell's class, and she got me a tutor. Now I'm doin' okay. Not great, but I'm passing. She was nice about it. Even old Pippin cut me some slack. Okay, I'm not smart. I don't study a lot. I hate school. But Buckingham's a real creep. I wish he'd go on one of those safaris and one of those endangered animals he's so crazy about would eat him up. That's what I wish."

"Look, Eric," Oliver reasoned. "How about this? At lunchtime on Mondays and Tuesdays, I'll meet you at the study area by Harriet Tubman's statue. I'll bring my sandwich and we can study science. The next test is on Chapter 7, erosion and river building, and we'll go over that good. We'll go over and over it, and you can pass the test."

Eric stared at Oliver. "You'd do that?" he asked.

"Yeah, sure," Oliver replied.

"Bro," Eric declared, "I swear to you I wasn't going into that classroom to steal any laptops or anything. I just wanted to get a copy of the test. I'm real sorry I hit you. I didn't mean to do that. I didn't hurt you too bad, did I?"

"No," Oliver answered, "I think I'll live. So am I going to see you at Harriet Tubman's statue at lunchtime tomorrow, Eric?"

"Yeah, I'll be there. Thanks. You're all right, man," Eric told him.

"Now get the devil out of here," Oliver ordered him.

Eric was gone so fast he seemed to have turned into the wind.

"I think I'm gonna cry," Alonee sighed.

"On my planet we highly value the quality of mercy," Oliver announced.

"Or maybe I'll just scream," Alonee said. "Come on, let's stop off at my house and I'll put something on your sore eyebrow."

"Won't your parents think you're dating a bum if I show up all bruised and bloody?" Oliver asked, as they walked toward the BMW.

"My parents are very understanding," Alonee said. "One day I brought home a wounded seagull and another time I brought home a chipmunk with a broken leg."

"Now, I'm in the same category as a wounded bird and chipmunk!" Oliver chuckled.

CHAPTER FIVE

When Alonee and Oliver got to her house, her mother was home, and her father was at the fire station. Her mother watched as Alonee washed the blood off Oliver's brow and applied an antibiotic salve and a small bandage.

"You are very good, Alonee," Mom noted. "You'll be a good mother. We mothers spend half our lives patching up our little boys." She then looked at Oliver. "If I ask you how you got hurt, you will probably tell me you ran into a door, but the truth is you were in a fight, weren't you? A mother can tell these things."

Oliver laughed. He said to Alonee, "I like your mom. She doesn't mince words. Yes, Mrs. Lennox, I was in a fight. This kid was trying to break into a classroom at Tubman to steal test papers, and I caught him. But after everything settled down, we talked and now we're friends."

Mom looked at Alonee. "This is all the truth?" she asked.

"I'm afraid so," Alonee affirmed.

After Oliver left to go home, Lark came up to her sister and cooed, "Oooooo, he's sooo cute, Alonee."

Alonee smiled at her sister. "I like him," she announced.

"Really, *really* like him?" Lark asked.

Alonee paused. She was having feelings about Oliver Randall that she never had for a boy other than Jaris. She thought about him as soon as she woke up in the morning and just before going to sleep at night. She kept picturing the way he looked when various things happened, the way he smiled, or laughed. "Maybe," Alonee finally responded.

On Monday, Oliver studied with Eric Carney. They spent the entire lunch hour going over how rain, water, and wind change landforms. Oliver made notes from the chapter and showed Eric how he high-lighted the important words from those notes with brightly colored felt pens. "I like pale orange or bright yellow highlighting," Oliver explained. "See Eric, the trick is to go over the notes every day, and they get into your brain. That way, when the test comes along, you don't go into a panic and forget everything."

Eric was cooperative and grateful. Then they both joined the stream of students heading for Mr. Buckingham's afternoon class. Oliver sat down, but Eric went up to the teacher's desk to explain how serious he was about studying now. He said he really wanted to do better in this class.

Mr. Buckingham stared at Eric and said dryly, "You're a very late convert to stu-diousness, young man. Your grade is so bad in this class that I doubt anything you do will be of much help now."

"But listen," Eric begged, a frantic tone to his voice, "I'm gonna really study and I know I can—"

"You've spent most of the semester reading automotive magazines, skillfully concealed in your textbook, Eric," Mr. Buckingham interrupted coldly. "Now, in the final hours you've mended your ways? I am a skeptic, but we shall see."

"I could still bring my grade up if I did okay on the last tests, right?" Eric asked. "I mean, it's possible, isn't it?"

"Excuse me, but I must really start class now," Mr. Buckingham announced, waving his hand at Eric dismissively. "I have much material to cover." He stood then and called the class to order as Eric went to his desk.

Eric had a terrible look on his face.

After class, Eric hurried out before Oliver could talk to him. Alonee was going to walk out with Oliver, and they were going to the vending machine for the beautiful oranges just stocked there. But instead Oliver walked up to the teacher's desk. Alonee lingered just outside the classroom, puzzled.

"Mr. Buckingham," Oliver began, "I know it's none of my business, but a guy like Eric needs a little bit of support now that he's trying to turn things around."

"You are absolutely correct," Mr. Buckingham replied. "It is none of your business."

"Sir," Oliver continued, "with all due respect—"

"No," Mr. Buckingham snapped, "with *no* respect whatsoever. You are disrespecting me enormously for even discussing another student with me. I have been teaching for thirty years and, if I do say so, quite successfully. How I deal with my students is none of your concern. Now, if you will excuse me to do my work, I will try to overlook your rude audacity."

Oliver left the classroom and joined Alonee. As they walked to the vending machine Oliver asked, "Man, did you hear that guy?" Oliver stuck the coins in the machine almost belligerently. Alonee had never seen him so steamed.

"Yes," Alonee said.

"What's *with* him? Who does he think he is?" Oliver snarled.

"His ancestors were kings in Africa," Alonee offered.

"So what? Mine were slaves in Louisiana, and they were just as good as him," Oliver growled. Dark anger flashed in his eyes. "I mean, the guy has to show a little compassion. I know Eric is a pain and he's been goofing off, but give the guy a ray of hope! Don't step on him like he's a bug!"

Alonee noticed Ryann and Leticia walking together again after lunch. Ryann gave Alonee a dirty look. Then, as their paths crossed, Ryann said in a catty voice, "I notice Oliver didn't eat lunch with you today. Maybe he's getting sick of being followed around by his little wannabe girlfriend. Did he break loose for one day?"

Alonee ignored Ryann, but she heard Leticia say in an exasperated voice, "Girl, you're just making a fool of yourself. The guy doesn't like you. Deal with it!"

"He hasn't had the chance to get to know me," Ryann whined. "She won't let go of him long enough to let him pick his own friends!"

"We're going down to the mall on Friday after school like we always do, aren't we Ryann?" Leticia asked.

"No!" Ryann snapped. "I'm tired of hanging with you all the time."

Alonee didn't hear what Leticia said, but later on in the day she was crying.

Alonee felt sorry for Leticia. In that little town in Alabama they clung to each other like sisters, Ryann and Leticia. Now they lived near a big city and everything was different. The trouble was that Ryann wanted more. She had outgrown the closeness of the friendship. She was totally into having a boyfriend now, and Leticia wasn't there yet. Leticia wasn't as pretty as Ryann, and she desperately wanted to hang on to her only friend. Alonee knew how she would feel if suddenly her little posse of friends wanted little to do with her anymore. Leticia must feel as if all that was warm and comforting from her childhood was getting away from her.

Alonee was walking from school after classes when she saw Leticia coming alone toward the bus stop. Alonee drew closer to her and said, "Hey Leticia, me and Sami Archer are going to the mall after school on Friday. Want to hang with us? There're some good sales in the stores, and I got some coupons I'll share with you."

Leticia seemed stunned. She stared at Alonee for a minute, then she said, "I wish that jerk Oliver Randall hadn't come here to school. He's ruined Ryann. She's gone crazy over him, and now she doesn't want to be my friend anymore."

Alonee shrugged and said, "Well, let us girls go shopping on Friday. Nothing makes a girl feel better than getting a good pair of jeans at half price."

"Jasmine's right," Leticia went on bitterly. "There's something evil about that Oliver Randall. He's up to something bad. If Ryann wasn't such a fool, she'd see that. I just wish he'd go away and things could be like they were before." Leticia turned and walked on toward the bus stop, not responding to Alonee's invitation to go shopping.

Mr. Wingate was very glad another junior signed up for the talent show. He met with Oliver and listened to him sing for a few minutes. "Ah," Mr. Wingate declared, "fantastic. A very good voice, young man. Really should be a great addition to the show. I'm in charge of this, you know, and it's not my favorite extracurricular activity. But at least we'll have one good performer."

Leaving the audition with Alonee at his side, Oliver was still upset about the way

Mr. Buckingham had treated Eric. He looked for him after school. Eric was nowhere to be found. On Tuesday, Eric didn't show up for school at all. Oliver was afraid that Mr. Buckingham had so totally discouraged him that he figured there was no sense in even trying.

"I wonder if anybody knows where the guy lives," Oliver commented to Alonee.

"Yeah, I think I do," Alonee replied. "He lives over on Indigo Street. Quincy Pierce lives there, and one day when we were over there I saw Eric in his yard. It's kind of a rundown neighborhood. The rents are cheaper over there because the landlords don't bother to fix anything."

After school, Trevor's older brother, Tommy, drove Oliver and Alonee over to Indigo Street. Alonee glanced at the row of frame and stucco houses and said, "That green house at the end of the street. I think Eric lives there."

They pulled up in front of the house. The front yard was dirt, with no sign that a lawn had ever been there. A few yellowing weeds stuck out of the ground. Several children, all younger than Eric, were playing with sticks and boxes in the dirt. Tommy waited in the car while Oliver and Alonee went to the door. It was open, covered by a broken screen. "Hi, anybody home?" Oliver called.

A woman with a baby on her hip appeared. She had clearly been crying. "Eric's not home," she announced. "You kids from school? Do you know where he is? He left the house for school this mornin'. Then a lady from the office down there called and said he didn' go to school. I'm scared he's run away or something."

"We're, uh, friends of his," Oliver explained. "I've been helping him bring up his grades in science. But he missed our session today, and I got worried."

"My husband's 'bout at the end of his rope with that boy," the woman went on. "My husband's at work now. He's gonna be so mad that the boy didn't go to school like he's supposed to. We're doin' the best that we can, but Eric, he is a problem child. My husband whups him up and down his head, but it don' do no good."

"He ever run away before?" Oliver asked.

"Yeah, he done that too," his mother answered. "I don' know what we can do to turn the boy 'round. One time he was gone a whole week. He was hiding under some freeway bridge. He was lookin' for food. His father whupped him so bad when he finally come home that the boy couldn' sit for a week. I thought that cured him, but looks like it didn'. What you going to do with such a boy? My husband is a good man. He loves his kids. He don' know what to do to straighten out that boy."

"Well," Alonee assured the mother, "we'll keep an eye out for him."

"If you see him, Mrs. Carney," Oliver said, "tell him Oliver was here looking for him. I still want to help him with science."

"I will sure tell him that," Mrs. Carney said. "And thank you for that."

As they walked to the car, Oliver made a comment. "You know my dad teaches in college, but he thinks there are a lot of kids who shouldn't be in high schools like Tubman. Kids like Eric shouldn't be learning history and biology. He should be learning a trade, right after middle school. Dad says years ago there were a lot more trade schools. Now everybody is pushed into general education. For some kids like Eric that just means a lot of frustration."

"Yeah," Alonee agreed. "It's not so much that Eric can't do the work, he just isn't interested. All he wants to do is read about cars."

"Yeah," Oliver added, "he doesn't give a rat's tail about erosion. He wants to know all about turbo engines."

Tommy dropped Oliver and Alonee off at their homes.

Alonee spent some time studying science herself. Mr. Buckingham gave hard tests, and even a good student like Alonee needed to study. Later, Alonee went out to water her mother's roses. They needed deep watering. There had been little rain this season. Alonee closely followed the water department rules about watering infrequently and deeply. But as she turned off the hose, she noticed the kids across the street soaking their driveway. Water, made shiny and oily from the lubricants on the blacktop, went bubbling toward the storm drain.

Alonee remembered Mr. Buckingham's stern face, and she strolled across the street. "Girls, you shouldn't be hosing down the driveway. You should use a broom. Look at all the dirty water going in the storm drain . . ."

"So what?" the ten-year-old replied.

"Look, Joy," Alonee explained, "see the picture of the duck on the curb? That means if you wash all that poison down the storm drains, it ends up in the sea and kills the ducks and other living things."

"I don't care," Joy declared. "Dad told me to hose down the driveway."

Just then Joy's father came out. He was a nice neighbor, friendly, helpful, a good father to his two children. "What's up, Alonee?" he asked with a big smile.

"I was just telling Joy that it's better to sweep the driveway," Alonee responded. "When you wash the oil and stuff down the driveway, it gets into the storm drain and goes into the waterways. We're studying about that in our science class at school, and it's really important."

"Ahhh, that's a lot of bunk," the father laughed. "Those teachers are full of it. They got all these wacky ideas, and they're scaring you poor kids out of your wits. We've *always* hosed down the driveway, and the world hasn't come to an end yet. It's a great big ocean, Alonee. A little oil and gunk doesn't matter."

"Well, our teacher is an environmentalist and—" Alonee began to say.

"They're the worst," the father announced. "They're nuts."

Alonee wasn't going to give up. "He is so passionate about not flushing pollutants down the storm drain that he called the police when his neighbor flushed a lot of poison down the drain."

"He did that to a neighbor?" The man was not smiling anymore. "Your teacher must be crazy. If a neighbor did that to me I'd bust him in the chops. You get the cops on your case and you're cooked!"

Alonee crossed the street and went back into her own house. Her neighbor was a lost cause. He was going to do what he wanted to do no matter what.

Alonee went into her bedroom and stretched out, looking up at the ceiling. Her father had painted all her favorite cartoon characters on the ceiling. He started when she was about six. There were Bambi, Cinderella, Nemo, and Miss Piggy. Several times Mom suggested painting over the cartoons and making something more appropriate for a sixteen-year-old girl, but

Alonee refused. It was not so much that she still loved the figures but that she loved the thought that Daddy had taken the time to put them there for her.

It was hard for Alonee to part with what was warm and comfortable. That's why she continued to look at Jaris Spain so lovingly. In her fantasies, Jaris and Sereeta would have a friendly breakup. Then Jaris would discover that he really loved Alonee as much as she had always loved him. Now the fantasy had faded suddenly. Something real and vital had taken its place—a boy named Oliver.

Alonee went to bed early Tuesday night. She had just fallen asleep when a sound roused her. At first it seemed part of a dream she was having. But it was loud and piercing, and she knew it was real.

Alonee sat up in bed, startled.

CHAPTER SIX

The screams of fire engine sirens ripped apart the silence of the night. Alonee's eyes opened wide. She scrambled from her bed and ran to the window. There were no brushy canyons around here, so there was no need to worry about a Santa Ana wind whipping a fire near town and forcing an evacuation.

Alonee's first thought was Tubman High School, but from the sound of the fire engines, they weren't going in that direction. They seemed to be heading toward the nice apartment buildings over on Algonquin Avenue.

Alonee turned on her television set. The news wasn't showing anything about a fire.

The radio news was also broadcasting its usual fare of shrill political voices. Alonee thought the fire was not serious if nobody was talking about it in the media. Then her mother came quietly into her bedroom.

"Mattie Archer just called me, Alonee," Mom said to her. "She says a car's burning on the next street from them. It's down by the apartments. Somebody set a parked car on fire, and when the flames reached the gas tank, it exploded. Nobody got hurt, though."

"Oh wow!" Alonee cried, "That's horrible. Does Sami's mom know whose car it is?"

"Yeah," Mom answered, "she says it's the only Toyota Prius in the neighborhood. It's driven by the science teacher at Tubman, Mr. Buckingham. You have him, don't you, sweetie? He always parks his car out front, and that's where they torched it."

Alonee turned numb. She thought immediately of Eric Carney. She remembered the hatred in his eyes on Monday when he walked back from Mr. Buckingham's desk, after the teacher told him his grades were probably too far gone for him to ever pass. Eric had run away. "He felt he had nothing to lose," Alonee thought. "And it was all Mr. Buckingham's fault."

"Why would somebody do such a terrible thing to Mr. Buckingham's car," Mom wondered. "I thought you kids liked him. He seems so brilliant. He was always very cordial when we met him during open houses."

"Yeah," Alonee agreed, "he's a good teacher, but he's a tough grader. He flunks a lot of kids."

"You mean to tell me there's a student at Tubman so vicious that he'd torch a teacher's car over a bad grade?" Mom groaned. "Lord in Heaven, what is this world coming to?"

"I'm glad nobody was hurt anyway," Alonee noted.

"Thank the Lord for that, but the poor man must be distraught," Mom declared.

"Imagine having something like that happen! Being woke up in the middle of the night to find your car on fire."

When Mom returned to her room, Alonee called Oliver. "Oliver, did you hear?" she asked him.

"Hear what?" he asked in a sleepy voice. "I've been asleep on the couch."

"Oh, I'm sorry I woke you up, Oliver," Alonee apologized. "I thought you heard the fire engines. Somebody burned up Mr. Buckingham's Toyota. Sami Archer's mom lives on the next street and her mom called my mom. Nobody was hurt, but the car is totally destroyed."

Oliver did not answer right away. Then he groaned, "Oh brother!"

"Yeah, are you thinking what I'm thinking, Oliver?" Alonee asked.

"Eric, huh? Wow," Oliver responded. "Maybe we should have called the cops when he was trying to break into Mr. Buckingham's classroom that day. You wanted to. You asked me if you should. Wow, this is bad, really bad. This isn't starting a little fire in a trash can. This is a felony."

"We're not sure he did it, but . . ." Alonee hesitated. "I mean somebody else could have it in for Mr. Buckingham. He's pretty harsh. He gave out four Fs in the last quarter. He once told the class he flunks more Tubman kids than any other teacher. He seemed kinda proud of that."

"Yeah, but—oh brother," was all Oliver could say. "Well, Alonee, thanks for telling me. Nothing we can do about it now. Try to get some sleep. I'll see you in the morning. Let's hope by then they found the vandal who burned the car."

Lark appeared in the doorway of Alonee's room. She was in her butterfly-covered pajamas. "Is something burning around here, Alonee?" she asked.

"It's way over on another street," Alonee told her. "It's a car. It's okay. No-body was hurt. Somebody set a car on fire."

"I'm scared of people who set fires!" Lark declared, her eyes wide. "You have to be a really bad person to set a fire on purpose. I hope the police find the bad people really fast."

"Yes," Alonee agreed. "You should go back to bed before Mom hears you."

After Lark went back to her room, Alonee tried to get back to sleep but couldn't for the rest of the night. The police would investigate this crime a lot more thoroughly than the trash can fire behind Mr. Buckingham's classroom. That might have been the result of someone's carelessness. This was a deliberate crime.

The police would interview Mr. Buckingham, and he would probably mention Eric as an angry student. He might give the police other names too. But Mr. Buckingham did not know about the day Eric tried to break into his classroom. Alonee and Oliver kept that a secret. Now Alonee wondered if they should tell the police about it. Telling would surely nail Eric . . .

Alonee kept recalling the hatred on Eric's face and his bitter words—"Buckingham . . . he's an old devil . . ."

On Wednesday morning, what had happened to Mr. Buckingham's Toyota was widely known.

"I'm not surprised," Jasmine commented. "Spooky stuff been happening around here. Just keep happening. I wouldn't be surprised if that new guy—Oliver—had something to do with all this stuff."

"That's the stupidest thing I ever heard," Sami scoffed. "Girl, you must stay in the sun too long. The heat's meltin' your brains."

Alonee felt strange. She actually liked Mr. Buckingham for his passion on the environment. She enjoyed him as a teacher. If you studied hard, you could make the grade in his class. But Oliver clearly had a problem with how Mr. Buckingham treated Eric.

"I wonder if Buckingham shows up this morning," Marko suggested. "I bet he's gonna be scared out of his wits and we get a sub. That's good, 'cause then we won't have the test."

"Look," Jasmine cried, "look at that shiny rental car just pulling into the teacher's parking lot! That's Mr. Buckingham getting out with his briefcase, strutting just like usual. Wow, that sucka is strong!"

"Nothin' can stop that dude," Derrick remarked with a trace of admiration, even though he struggled hard in the science class to pull a C.

"But he's got to be spooked," Marko insisted. "Somebody after him. If some dude barbecued my wheels, I think I'd go into hibernation for a while."

Mr. Buckingham ignored the group of students gathered outside his classroom. He didn't even look in their direction. He went into his classroom as usual and locked the door behind him. He usually arrived early and spent about twenty minutes preparing for the day. He didn't want students interrupting him. Ms. McDowell came early too, but students were always welcome when she was there. Mr. Pippin always came in very shortly before the bell.

The first class was English, and nobody in Mr. Pippin's class wanted to talk about Shakespeare.

"You think there's a plot against the teachers here at Tubman?" Marko asked, as Mr. Pippin dropped his briefcase on his desk.

"What are you talking about?" Mr. Pippin asked wearily.

"Just last night, Mr. Pippin. Didn't you hear? Somebody burned up Mr. Buckingham's car," Jasmine chimed in.

Mr. Pippin looked shocked. "Last night?" he gasped.

"Yeah," Marko answered. "They set fire to his Toyota that was parked in front of his apartment. Burned it to a crisp. I thought you knew about that."

"Some people think there's bad stuff goin' on here, Mr. Pippin," Jasmine added ominously. "Like maybe there's a curse on Tubman High School or something."

"Don't be ridiculous," Mr. Pippin replied in a shaky voice. "It's most unfortunate that such vandalism occurs, but that's all it is. Scoundrels who have nothing better to do than shoot out streetlights or set fires. They are out there doing their mischief. It has nothing to do with Tubman High School."

"I don't know," Jasmine persisted. "Fire in the trash can and now this."

"It's kind of funny," Marko remarked. "Mr. Buckingham drives a Toyota Prius, and that's good for the environment. Now here it gets burned up, filling the neighborhood with smoke. Kinda ironic, huh, Mr. Pippin?" Marko chuckled a little.

"It's not funny, Marko," Mr. Pippin told him. "Arson is never funny."

Later, after Mr. Pippin's class, Alonee got a chance to talk to Oliver alone. She confided, "I've been worried that we know something nobody else knows. I mean, what should we do if the police come around? Should we tell them what happened on Sunday?"

Oliver frowned. "I've been thinking about that too. I'm going back and forth on it. All that Eric did was try to break into the science classroom to get some tests. I mean, yeah, he hates Buckingham. Buckingham knows Eric doesn't like him. He'll tell that to the police. I don't think we need to add to the kid's problems by piling something else on, Alonee."

Alonee nodded. "I'll go along with that. I keep hoping it's not Eric, but it looks bad. Eric is such a loser and now he doesn't even have a home. A sixteen-year-old guy living on the street, scrounging for food, for someplace to sleep. I see grown men out there, sleeping on pieces of cardboard on cold nights, but he's a kid." She sighed.

"Yeah," Oliver agreed. He grasped Alonee's hand and gave it a little squeeze. "I hear you, babe." Then they went to their separate classes. Later, they would both be in Mr. Buckingham's class.

Mr. Buckingham made no mention of his car. He passed out the tests as usual. Then he patrolled the aisles, making sure nobody was copying answers. That was an automatic F in his class. Nobody could tell from his demeanor that anything out of the ordinary had happened to him last night.

After class, Leticia muttered, "He's not even human."

"Maybe he's a humanoid," Marko suggested. "They got no feelings."

"He's got feelings," Jaris stated. "It's just that he holds himself tightly under control. He keeps it all bottled up inside him, but maybe that's not healthy. My pop explodes all the time. He said it's like a tea kettle. You need these little explosions or one day you'll shatter into a million pieces."

In the late afternoon, the buzz around Tubman High was that Mr. Buckingham had given the police the names of all his students who he felt had grudges against him. They had either failed his class or were now failing. The year before, Mr. Buckingham had flunked twenty students. In one case, a frantic mother appeared to tell Mr. Buckingham that, because of the F in science, her son had failed to gain entrance to a four-year college. When the angry woman wouldn't leave, Mr. Buckingham had called security. She had to be escorted off the campus. Another failed student had been so angry that she threatened to malign Mr. Buckingham on her Web site. And then there was Eric Carney and the ones he was flunking this year.

Alonee called the Carney home after school. "Have you heard from Eric at all?" she asked.

"No," Mrs. Carney said sadly. "The police were here asking questions about some fire. They said there was a teacher at Tubman High whose car was burned up. I told 'em that has nothin' to do with my son. He never had any trouble with teachers. He never talked about this man the police mentioned—a Mr. Buckman or somethin'

like that. I told the police that my son is
missing, and they have to find him before
he's hurt. But they seemed more interested
in the fire."

"Well, I hope Eric comes home soon,
Mrs. Carney," Alonee consoled her.

"You know what my husband is doing
right now? He's sittin' there cryin' like a
baby." Mrs. Carney was speaking with a sob
in her voice. "He is so worried. He loves the
boy. He really does. Eric is our firstborn.
When he had to whup him, he'd always say
it hurt him more than it hurt Eric, and that
was the truth. My husband isn' one of these
men who don't care for their children. No
ma'am. He loves that boy."

That evening, Oliver Randall joined
the other students who were practicing for
the talent show in the auditorium. Carissa
Polson sang a nice blues song, and Oliver
sang an old classic, "Bridge Over Troubled
Water" by Simon and Garfunkel. Alonee
joined in the applause. When Oliver

stepped off the stage, Ryann Kern came running up to him. Ryann was helping out backstage. "Oh, Oliver, that was wonderful!" she cooed.

"Why thank you, Ryann," Oliver responded.

"Oh, I'm so happy you're in the talent show. You're so good," Ryann continued. "You could be a professional singer. You could make records and make a ton of money." Ryann stood squarely in front of Oliver so that he couldn't get down the steps. Finally he got around her and joined a group of friends, including Alonee, Sami, and Jaris.

"You were good, dude," Sami congratulated him.

"I'm nervous," Oliver admitted.

The four of them walked out into the darkness. Sami had to get home, so she said goodnight. The teacher's parking lot was empty except for Ms. McDowell's pickup truck. Her brother, Shane "Sparky" Burgess, was leaning against it, waiting for

THE QUALITY OF MERCY

her to come out of her classroom. She had been tutoring a student.

Oliver had been telling Jaris and Alonee that he was trying to find Eric Carney. Now Jaris pointed toward the truck. "Hey! Sparky might be able to help you. He was living in those homeless hang-outs for a while."

The three of them approached the boy.

"Hey Sparky," Jaris called, "you still practicing with the baseball?"

"Yeah," the boy said with a grin. "When I come back to Tubman, coach says I might get a spot on the varsity team."

"Sparky," Jaris said, "my friend here is looking for a runaway kid in trouble. Do you know anyplace around here where he might be hanging out?"

"I know my favorite place was a little ravine over on Pequot Street," Sparky offered. "Lot of runaway kids go there. You go down into a ravine, and you can't be seen from the street. You can stretch a tarp

110

across the tops of the trees and get a lot of protection from the weather."

"Thanks, Sparky," Oliver said. "And one more thing—your sister is the best teacher here at Tubman. Everybody respects her and loves her too. She's amazing."

"Me too," Sparky agreed, his grin widening. "I love my big sister a lot."

CHAPTER SEVEN

About an hour after talking with Sparky, the three of them—Alonee, Jaris, and Oliver—headed for the ravine in the BMW. As they drove down to Pequot Street, the night was dark with a moon creeping slowly from the clouds.

"I remember the place Sparky was talking about," Jaris noted. "I bet you do too, Alonee. When we were in fifth grade, we'd go down there and pretend we were explorers."

"Yeah," Alonee recalled. "I remember there were berries growing down there, and one time we had a feast."

"Used to be a little creek down there in the winter, and we'd hunt for pollywogs," Jaris added. "Remember, Alonee?'

"Yeah," she replied. Jaris seemed to be looking at her more than usual. He had a sort of pensive look in his eyes.

They parked on the street and slowly made their way down into the ravine. The soil was loose and slippery. "I see some tarps," Oliver observed. "And I smell smoke . . . and weed."

"Eric!" Oliver called out. "We're your friends from school. We just want to make sure you're okay." Nobody answered. The trio moved closer, and suddenly someone bolted from under a tarp and ran away.

"There he is," Oliver pointed, sprinting after Eric. "Hey dude! Not to worry. We just want to talk to you," Oliver shouted.

Eric stopped and turned slowly. He looked dirty and disheveled. "I didn't burn up the old devil's car," he said, panting, in an exhausted voice. "I heard about it. They're blaming me, aren't they?"

113

"No," Oliver told him. "The police talked to Buckingham, and he gave them lots of names of disgruntled students who don't like the guy."

"Yeah, but I bet they're thinkin' it's probably me," Eric insisted.

"Eric," Alonee said, catching up with the two boys, "you make yourself look guilty by hiding out like this. You need to go home." Oliver was a little nervous about Alonee coming along, but she had insisted.

"My old man'll kill me," Eric claimed.

"No, he won't," Alonee protested. "I talked to your mom. She said your father's crying like a baby he's so worried about you. I know he's been rough on you, Eric, but he loves you."

"They'll arrest me and stick me with that arson charge," Eric rattled on, sounding panicky.

Oliver drew closer. "Look bro," he said, "you said you didn't do it. I believe you. Maybe you did do it, and I'm a fool, but I really do believe you. I think you're the kind of a guy who'd scrawl bad words on somebody's fence if you were mad at them, but you wouldn't tear down the fence. I think you should go home. The cops have a lot of evidence from the fire. It won't point to you if you're innocent. I think you are. You need to go home and tell your folks you're sorry. If your father whups you, well, then that's a whole 'nother thing you have to work out with him. Besides, as wrong as that whuppin' might be, you're better off at home than hanging around here."

"I'm s-so s-scared," Eric stammered.

"Eric," Oliver asserted. "Trust me, man. I'm giving you good advice. Go home. Go back to school. We can study together again. I'll help you through this, man. We can salvage that class with a C. You still got a chance, Eric. Go home. Take a nice hot shower. Your mom will make you a good, hot meal. If you stay here, you'll be cold and dirty and eating scraps. Your parents'll be tearing their hair out worrying. Eric, you got a way of getting home?"

"My bike . . . I got my bike," Eric answered. "But . . ."

"You want a ride home, Eric?" Oliver asked.

"No," he said. "I, uh . . . got my bike."

The trio went back up the hill to the street. Oliver had a faint smile on his face. "I think he's going home," he said.

Alonee smiled at Oliver. "You're good, Oliver. You have a way about you."

Alonee told Oliver she would find out what happened with Eric and let him know. Later that night, Alonee called the Carney home.

"I'm one of Eric's friends," Alonee said, "and I was wondering . . ."

The mother sounded like she had been crying. "He come home!" she cried over the phone, "Oh praise the Lord, our boy come home! And his daddy is going easy on him. Praise the Lord!"

"I'm so glad, Mrs. Carney," Alonee said.

"Oh," Mrs. Carney added, "and will you tell this boy Oliver—tell him that Eric says thanks. Will you do that?"

"I sure will, right away," Alonee assured her. She called Oliver the moment she hung up and told him the good news. She heard him yelling it to his father. "Dad! The kid went home! He really did!" Then, to Alonee, Oliver said, "Oh man, that's great news. Thanks, Alonee. I think we'll see Eric in the morning."

When Alonee arrived at school the next morning, she noticed Jaris Spain standing alongside Harriet Tubman's statue. He was waiting for Alonee. Alonee's heart leaped. She wasn't sure what this would be about, but she was nervous.

"Hi Alonee," Jaris called. "I've been waiting to talk to you."

"Hi Jaris," Alone said. "Oh, good news about Eric. He went home last night just like Oliver thought he would, and his dad isn't beating on him."

"Oh yeah, that's great," Jaris responded. "Oliver really convinced him that was the right thing to do. You gotta hand it to Oliver." Then Jaris got to the point. "Uh, Alonee, I wanted to ask you something. It's none of my business, but I care about you. I'll always care about you." He seemed uneasy and nervous.

"What's up, Jaris?" Alonee asked.

"You and Oliver are getting really close, aren't you?" Jaris finally noted.

"Well, we like each other a lot," Alonee answered. "I guess you could say we are getting close."

"Well, it just struck me the other day. I thought, 'Wow, Alonee's in love with somebody . . . Alonee . . . ,'" Jaris said, his voice a little thin.

"You know what attracted me to Oliver, Jaris?" Alonee found herself admitting. "In the beginning he reminded me of you. I've always . . . I mean, I've always thought you were special. You've been special to me for a long time. Couldn't you tell, Jaris?"

"Yeah, and you've been special to me too," Jaris confided.

"Sort of like a really nice sister," Alonee added, smiling.

"Alonee," Jaris said, "he's better than me. He's way better than me. I've always had my demons. I'm my pop's son. We're always waiting for the next shoe to drop with him. We got this way of horribalizing life. Like there's a darkness out there, and we're running as fast as we can because it wants to overtake us. Oliver is solid. He's much better than me, Alonee."

"Not better, Jaris," Alonee pointed out, "just different. A girl never forgets her first love, especially one as cute and sweet as you are, Jaris Spain."

"I just wanted you to know something, Alonee," Jaris told her, in a voice that shook a little, like a reed in the wind. "I like Oliver and I think he's a good guy. And I'm really happy for you. You deserve the best."

Alonee reached for Jaris's shoulders and brought him down to where she could kiss him. When she drew back, she could see tears in his eyes. She felt tears in her own eyes. "Like the song says," Alonee whispered, " 'I will always love you' . . . right?"

Jaris nodded and replied, "Me too, babe." Then he turned and walked away.

Alonee walked toward her first class. "Was that goodbye?" she wondered. It felt like good-bye to her, but she wasn't sad.

They would see each other many times, maybe throughout their lives if things turned out like that. So maybe the goodbye was to a dream, to a fantasy—Alonee's fantasy. It had flickered out and died like a flame that had burned too long. And that was a good thing because another new flame was coming to life. It brought a rush of happiness to Alonee Lennox every time she thought about it. His name was Oliver Randall.

Before Alonee reached American history, her first period class that day, she ran into Derrick Shaw.

"Hey Alonee, you look happy," he noted.

"I guess so," Alonee responded. "Things are going pretty good."

Derrick and Alonee both looked over toward the teacher's parking lot. As Mr. Buckingham was arriving, he dropped his briefcase, it burst open, and papers flew all over. It was a strange, disconcerting sight to see him stooping to retrieve his papers. He seemed very agitated.

"Things ain't goin' so good for him, huh?" Derrick commented. "I guess one of his students got so mad at him that they burned up his car. It was a nice car too. A Prius."

"That was such a horrible thing to do," Alonee said. "I can't imagine someone doing that."

Derrick shrugged his shoulders. "Well, maybe it wasn't even someone from here. Maybe he's got personal problems . . . in the family, you know."

"I don't know anything about his family," Alonee admitted. "He never talks about them."

"I seen his wife once," Derrick recalled. "His old car was in the garage, and she brought him to work. She's a lot like him. Very prim and proper. I think she teaches too. I sure feel bad for Mr. Buckingham. I'd feel awful if somebody burned up my car, if I *had* a car, that is. I'm lucky to have a bike. My daddy said if I'm ever to have a car, I better pay for it myself, 'cause with the family finances, they won't be givin' out cars real soon."

"Me too," Alonee replied. "My dad earns pretty good money at the fire department. But there are four of us kids, and Mom doesn't work. Money's tight. Oh! Derrick, look! There's Eric Carney riding up on his bike. He came back to school!"

"Yeah," Derrick said, "here he comes all right."

Marko was standing there. He looked at Eric as he locked up his bike. "That's the

dude that went missing right after Buckingham's wheels got roasted."

Jasmine laughed. "I wondered why that
dude jumped ship. Maybe he got his little
hands burned setting a fire," she suggested.

"Maybe he wanted to air the smoke
smell out of his jeans," Marko joked,
laughing too.

"We don't know who burned up Mr.
Buckingham's car," Alonee asserted coldly.
"Let's not be spreading rumors, Marko."

Marko laughed and looked at Derrick,
"Even a guy as dumb as you knows who
did it—right, Derrick? I mean, Eric was
begging at old Buckingham's feet on
Monday. The guy was almost on his knees.
We all saw it." Marko imitated Eric in an
exaggerated way. "'Oh please, teacher
man. I'll study my head off. I can do better.
Oh say I got a chance, please, pretty
please.' But old Bucky has a heart of
stone, so he kicks the dude in the teeth.
Eric's simmerin' with rage. He takes off.
Then while he's missing in action, Bucky's

Prius gets the torch. Like you need to be a rocket scientist for that to add up?"

"That's called circumstantial evidence," Oliver Randall stated, approaching the group and overhearing their conversation. Alonee had not even seen Oliver come up. "Circumstantial evidence is not hard evidence."

"Yeah?" Marko snapped. "Who do *you* think did it? Maybe you had something to do with it, Oliver. Nobody knows where you really came from, dude. All of a sudden you pop up here at Tubman with some crazy story about an old astronomy professor Dad and a diva Mom. *Who are you really dude?* Maybe you got some hidden agenda for stirring up trouble here at Tubman."

Most people, Alonee thought, would have gotten angry at Marko's charges, but Oliver just laughed and said, "Okay, you got me, Marko. You were right from the beginning. I'm from the Alpha Centauri system. My leaders sent me here to cause trouble at Tubman High School. They didn't tell me exactly why they wanted me to do that, but my leaders are kinda crazy. But then most leaders in the universe are a little wacky, right?"

Derrick laughed and looked at Marko. "He's making fun of you, man," he chuckled.

Marko glared at Derrick and stomped off, with Jasmine close behind. Oliver walked toward Eric, who was coming from the bike rack. "Hey man, good to see you. Remember, we study at noon."

"Yeah," Eric responded. "Thanks . . . uh . . . for everything."

"Everything cool at home, dude?" Oliver asked.

"Yeah, you were right, Oliver," Eric said. "My dad was . . . okay."

At midday, police investigators came on campus to interview several people, including the three students Mr. Buckingham was failing. They wanted to know where the students were when the Prius was set on fire. All but Eric were home with their families. Eric had already gone to the ravine, and he had no alibi.

When Eric came to study with Oliver and Alonee, he was petrified with fear. "I felt like they think it was me setting that fire," Eric said. "Oh man, I got no way to prove I wasn't over on Algonquin Avenue."

"Cool down," Oliver told him, "you've got no criminal record."

"Yeah . . . I sorta do," Eric admitted. "Last year I broke into a house. It was one of those foreclosures, you know. Nobody was there for a long time. I busted in and took some stuff. Not big stuff, but, you know, I got caught and had to go before this judge. I was fifteen. I hadn't turned sixteen yet. Anyway, the judge gave me probation. He said my record would be covered up 'cause I was a minor, but if I did anything else, everything'll come out."

"You'll be okay, Eric," Oliver said. "Just focus on studying for science and your other classes."

When the lunch hour ended, Alonee and Oliver were walking together to their next class. A terrible thought came to Alonee's mind. "What if Eric did set fire to that car?" she wondered. "We can't be sure he didn't."

"I know," Oliver agreed. "I've thought of that too. I don't think so but . . ." Oliver reached over and put his arm around Alonee's shoulders. "On my planet you are innocent until proven guilty."

Alonee smiled and replied, "On my planet too."

Alonee was nervous about Eric showing up for Mr. Buckingham's class for the first time since that Monday. The teacher had to know that the boy hated him and may well have destroyed his beloved car. How could Mr. Buckingham act civilly toward Eric? How could he hide the turmoil that was probably in his mind?

Three students had missed the Wednesday test. Before class, they turned in notes explaining their absences. Two of them showed Mr. Buckingham their notes from the doctors. All Eric had was a note from his father stating that he had "nervous headaches." Mr. Buckingham read the three notes and handed them back while saying nothing. Then he began his lecture on rain forests.

"Tropical rain forests are one of the basic life support systems of earth," Mr. Buckingham intoned. "They profoundly affect rainfall all over the world. This fact is all the more critical when one considers that fifty million acres of rain forest are destroyed every year in the world. This has ominous long-term consequences for us. Since there is more money to be made by destroying the rain forests than by preserving them, the future looks grim."

When Mr. Buckingham's lecture finished, he referred to makeup exams. "As you all know, I require proof of illness when you are absent from a test. Two of you provided doctor's reports. Anita, Robert, you may take the makeup exam next Tuesday." He then turned to Eric Carney. Eric was visibly shaking.

CHAPTER SEVEN

"Your father makes a riveting case for this nervous malady you allegedly suffer from, Eric," Mr. Buckingham stated, un-smiling. "I am not totally convinced. However, if you appear after school on Tuesday, you may take the makeup test."

"T-thanks, Mr. Buckingham," Eric replied, hurrying from the classroom like someone just released from death row.

When they were outside the classroom, Oliver told Eric, "Now we gotta really study, man."

"Yeah," Eric agreed. "I'll sure try, but did you notice how he was sneering at me? He doesn't give me much of a chance to pass. He can't wait for me to blow that test on Tuesday."

"Stifle that bad attitude man," Oliver demanded. "You hear what I'm saying? This isn't about Mr. Buckingham. It's about you. You study like mad and you believe in yourself. Don't waste your energy hating the man. Prove him wrong. You go do an awesome job on the test."

CHAPTER EIGHT

After classes that same day, Oliver had to stay late for another talent show rehearsal. Alonee sat in the audience, enjoying Oliver's singing. Then they left together.

Oliver's father was going to pick Oliver and Alonee up, and the three of them were going out for dinner. Alonee thought Oliver's father wanted to meet this girl his son seemed so interested in.

As they walked toward the front of the school where the BMW was scheduled to pick them up, Alonee noticed a man lurking behind the science building. She wasn't sure if it was a man or a boy, and immediately she thought of Eric. A chill ran down her spine. Eric was sure Mr. Buckingham was out to get him, even though the teacher was giving him another chance on the test.

"Oliver," Alonee pointed out, "some guy is over there behind the science building. It's too dark to make out who it is. Probably maintenance."

"Let's go check," Oliver replied. "I've noticed that they've been having trouble with the sprinkler system. With this drought, they want them to make every drop count."

Alonee and Oliver walked around to the back of the science building. An older man was standing there, scratching his stubble of a beard.

"Hi," Oliver greeted. "You trying to fix the sprinkler system? It's been doing a better job of watering the sidewalks than the lawns."

"Gophers," the man answered. "Darned gophers. They dig under the pipes, play havoc with the pipes."

Alonee looked at the man with the thin mustache and receding hairline more closely. He wore jeans, a nice shirt, and dress shoes. He didn't look like a maintenance worker. Isaac, the regular school maintenance man, wore heavy work shoes and overalls. This man was too well dressed.

"Oh, yeah," Oliver commented. "Mr. Buckingham's been complaining about the leaks and losing all that water. I think he said maintenance was having trouble fixing the lines."

"Oh, he's a complainer, all right," the man said with a wry grin. "Sam's been after me to stop the leaks because he can't stand seeing any natural resources wasted. If you kids are in his class, you know what a bear he is about the environment."

Alonee relaxed a little. This man was apparently a friend of Mr. Buckingham's. He called him by his first name, and few people did. "Yes sir, we know that about him. So can you get it fixed?" Alonee asked.

"I'd better," the man asserted jovially. "Would you want to face Sam Buckingham

without getting the job done? He always
calls on me when the regular guy around
here can't make the fix. We're old friends.
. . . Yep, Sam believes he can singlehand-
edly reverse progress and return the world
to an innocent and primitive state." He
laughed and continued prowling around the
lawn, kicking at raised clumps of grass and
muttering, "Darn gophers."

"What's your name, sir?" Oliver asked
curiously.

"Bob," he answered. "My slogan is
'Get Bob for the Job.'" He laughed again
and then said, "Gotta get more tools." He
headed for a green pickup parked in the
teacher's lot, his thin mustache twitching.

Oliver had only a moment to reflect on
what had just happened. Something just
didn't seem right.

Then he turned suddenly and said,
"There's my dad."

They rode in the BMW to a little buffet
restaurant near Tubman. The place wasn't
what Alonee expected. She thought an

133

astronomy professor like Louis Randall would choose more exotic food, like sushi or Thai. But as they walked in, Mr. Randall said, "I love this place. I like the idea of picking out what I like and in the amount I can handle. In the regular restaurants they give me way too much food, and I end up taking home a doggie bag. Then I never eat it because it never tastes as good the second day."

As they went down the buffet line, Alonee picked a chicken salad and fruit. "My dad likes this place too," Alonee remarked. "Good down-to-earth food."

Oliver and his father both picked fish and salad. As the trio sat down, Mr. Randall smiled at Alonee. "So you're the young lady Oliver has been talking so much about. We met once before, but I thought it was time to get to know one another. Oliver tells me you have three siblings."

"Yes, two sisters and a little brother," Alonee answered. Oliver's dad had a kind, time-lined face. Oliver had said he was seventy, so he was older than Alonee's grandfather, who was fifty-seven. Alonee never met anyone with a seventy-year-old father.

"It's lovely to have a big family," Mr. Randall commented. "My wife and I dote on this magnificent son of ours. The truth is we never planned on having children at all. Oh my, no. I met my wife when I was fifty-two years old. I was a curmudgeonly professor quite content with my solitary life. Katrina was a thirty-five-year-old opera singer, delighted with her career. I made the terrible mistake of attending *Madam Butterfly,* and I fell in love." He laughed and there was a twinkle in his eye. "I'm almost twenty years older than she is, yet she loved me."

Mr. Randall continued, smiling through it all. "When we married, I was into my science, and she was into her music. There was no place for children in our lives. In what turned out to be a blessing, Katrina was expecting in the first year! How could we cope with it? We were alarmed. Ah, but

Alonee, for me and for Katrina this child we did not plan on became the most wonderful, the most magical triumph in our lives. He is more awesome than any celestial event I have ever marveled over, more thrilling than Katrina's finest aria. Now neither of us can imagine a world without Oliver in it."

"That's beautiful!" Alonee remarked. She looked at Oliver. He was smiling as if he was hearing the story for the first time, though no doubt he had heard it often.

"Oliver has spent more time with Katrina than with me," Mr. Randall went on, "but now that he's here, it's my turn. And, of course, in the summers we vacation together, our strange little family. So Alonee, now you know where this young man of yours comes from. I do hope you don't find us too strange."

Alonee started giggling. She couldn't help herself. Oliver caught on right away and explained her reaction to his father. "Actually Dad," Oliver turned toward his father, "there's this guy at school, and he thinks maybe I'm an alien from another planet. He and his mom listen to this far-out radio program where people call in and say aliens are living among us. This guy, he thinks I'm an ET."

"Fascinating," Mr. Randall commented. "I listen to that program too sometimes when I can't sleep. You learn all sorts of things, about Big Foot and such. I doubt that the government hid those little alien bodies at Roswell, but I can't be so arrogant as to claim I know all the answers either. But Oliver—an ET? Hilarious!"

"You know," Mr. Randall continued, changing the subject, "I like this neighborhood around your high school, Alonee. It's real. It reminds me of the school I went to eons ago. I grew up in Watts. Came from an old-fashioned family and we lived on soul food, grits, and fried chicken. Even now I cook for myself, and I'm apt to eat too much fried chicken, and I can bake a mean sweet potato pie. And I love basketball.

Don't bother me when the basketball championships are on. I mean, a lot of years ago you'd have seen me, a skinny black kid jumping around on the park court. Not too good, but having the time of my life."

Alonee thought Oliver's father was delightful. She had been nervous thinking about spending time with him, but now she knew why Oliver was so special.

When Alonee got home, she told her parents about Louis Randall. "He's so real and warm and funny," Alonee reported. "I can see where Oliver gets his personality. And I see why he seems a little older than the other guys at Tubman. Having a dad who's older has made him more mature."

Later on that evening, Alonee's father asked, "Has there been any more trouble in that poor Mr. Buckingham's life? First that trash fire at his classroom, then his car is torched. The poor man must be getting a complex."

"The police talked to some students at school," Alonee replied, "the ones

138

Mr. Buckingham is flunking. I don't know if they came up with anything. Mr. Buckingham is a really brilliant teacher. He's interesting too. But he doesn't show a lot of mercy on kids who are having trouble with the material."

"Well, I sure hope they find the jerk who burned that car," Mr. Lennox said. "Anybody who'd do that is a dangerous person and needs to be taken off the streets."

On Friday morning when Alonee arrived at school, there was a big commotion. Police were gathered around the science building, and the area was cordoned off. The first person Alonee saw was Ms. McDowell. "What's going on, Ms. McDowell?" Alonee asked.

"Alonee, go to the auditorium," Ms. McDowell directed her. "All students with first period science are being sent there."

As students were coming onto the campus, the public address system was giving them the same message that Alonee got from Ms. McDowell. When the auditorium was full, Mr. Hawthorne, the vice principal, appeared. "We want you all to be calm," he began. "There isn't going to be any evacuation of the school. As soon as this problem is resolved and the police have gathered evidence, classes will continue as usual. What happened was probably a stupid prank. Someone left a large cardboard box just behind the science building. Of course, the police had to make sure there were no explosives or anything of that kind in the box. The box turned out to be full of harmless swamp snakes. Animal control is now in the process of taking them away."

"Snakes! Oh-my-gosh!" Jasmine screamed. "Did any of them get out?" Jasmine started looking frantically around the floor of the auditorium.

"No, no," Mr. Hawthorne assured everyone, "there's no reason for alarm of any kind. It appears all the snakes remained in the box where they were discovered early this morning by maintenance."

"I want to go home," Ryann cried out. "I hate snakes. Who did this? I'm terrified of snakes. I want to go home right now!"

"If any students feel so distressed that they want to call their parents to come and pick them up, we'll make arrangements for that," Mr. Hawthorne told the students. "But there's no need for panic. Outside the auditorium door you will find a listing of substitute classrooms we'll be using for science classes this morning. Consult the listing, and go to your usual science class in the substitute room. The police will be completing their investigation this morning. We expect everything will be back to normal in the afternoon. Thank you for your cooperation."

When Alonee and her fellow science students went to the substitute classroom, they were surprised to find that Mr. Buckingham wasn't there.

"They finally spooked the old fool," Marko declared. "The trash can fire didn't get him, the barbecuing of his Prius didn't

141

scare him off, but a box of swamp snakes did the trick."

Alonee glanced over at Eric Carney. He looked strange. He didn't seem shocked or even surprised. He just sat there, staring at the empty teacher's desk, looking at the podium where Mr. Buckingham would ordinarily be standing. When a substitute teacher, a middle-aged woman, came in, Eric brightened. With no preparation, she spent the class talking about El Niño and the drought.

"El Niño is the weather system that brings rain, and we hope it arrives this year to relieve our terrible drought. It would be refreshing indeed," she said, launching into her lecture.

At the end of the class, as the substitute was leaving, the students gathered outside the classroom. Eric remarked, "Be 'refreshing' if she got to be our regular teacher, huh?"

Jaris Spain ignored Eric's comment and said, "Somebody who saw the box before they carted it away said there was a message scrawled on it. It said, 'Here are some of your endangered species, you crazy fanatic.'"

"Wow!" Alonee gasped. "Somebody's really out to get Mr. Buckingham one way or another."

Eric was standing there in silence. Then he said, "It'd be good if he was gone. That lady we had today, she seemed nice. Buckingham's too mean. He shouldn't be a teacher. I didn't do any of the stuff that's been happening, but whoever did is doing us all a big favor. I'd like that lady to be our regular teacher. She looks like my mom."

"You sure you aren't the one behind all this, dude?" Marko asked Eric.

"No. I didn't do anything," Eric asserted, "I wouldn't even know where to find snakes like that. If I could find 'em, maybe I woulda thought about doing it. Ah! I wouldn't do it anyway. But I'm glad he's gone."

Oliver had a pained look on his face as he glanced at Eric. Alonee could tell he was having second thoughts about Eric's innocence. He was, in fact, wondering again if he and Alonee made the right decision that Sunday afternoon when they didn't report Eric trying to break into Mr. Buckingham's classroom. Maybe he wasn't just looking for tests to steal. Maybe he was planning to start a fire. Maybe they should have gone to the police right then and there and let them decide what to do. Maybe they had been too generous in accepting Eric's claims of innocence.

Alonee was having second thoughts too. If Eric was the vandal doing all these terrible things, then they could all have been prevented by reporting him.

"Eric," Oliver asked, "why are you so happy Mr. Buckingham is gone? He's letting you take the makeup test. Doesn't that count for anything?"

"He woulda flunked me on the makeup anyway," Eric objected. "Guys like me never have a chance with a teacher like Buckingham. He's a lot like those snakes in the box. He likes to wrap himself around things and crush them."

Sami Archer came along then. "You guys heard?" she asked. She had a very serious look on her face.

"Heard what?" Alonee answered, wondering what new calamity had struck.

"Mr. Buckingham," Sami explained. "He's in the hospital. They took him this morning by ambulance. He's gone to the ER. Might be a heart attack. My mom went over there. His wife called her. His wife real upset, hysterical. All this been too much. He's not a young man. This is pretty awful business, dudes."

"Did he get sick because of the snakes in the box by his classroom?" Jaris asked.

"Dunno," Sami replied, "but somebody from school called him early this morning and told him what was goin' on and soon after that, he was gettin' chest pains. His wife, she says he wanted to come to school as usual and teach his class. But the pains, they got worse, and he couldn't breathe, and Mom

told his wife they gotta call nine-one-one."
Sami shook her head grimly. "Whoever doin'
this, they mighta just killed a man."

Eric said nothing. He just stood there
with a blank look on his face. Finally he
announced, "It's nothin' to me."

"You're cold, Eric," Sami scolded.

"Buckingham didn't care about me,"
Eric protested, "Why should I care about
him? I didn't do anything to hurt him. You
want me to put on an act that I care about
him? Well, I don't." Eric walked away.

Alonee was on her way to her next
class when she heard Mr. Pippin and
Ms. McDowell talking outside on the little
patio by the teacher's lounge. Alonee felt
bad eavesdropping, but she couldn't resist.

"I warned Sam about his harshness
toward them," Mr. Pippin was saying. "I
certainly dislike many of them myself, but
you can't crush and dismiss them. I think
Sam doesn't care for people. He thinks
they're ruining the environment. I believe
he takes that attitude out on his students. As

awful as some of these kids can be, you can't just ruthlessly fail them. You can't take away their hope."

"I don't think he graded unfairly," Ms. McDowell responded. "Just very strictly. Like he wouldn't grade on the curve. If everybody got less than a certain percentage, he'd flunk everyone."

"Well, I'm going to the hospital now," Mr. Pippin stated. "I owe that to him. We've been colleagues here for what—thirty years? My gosh, has it been that long? You're young, Torie. The grind isn't wearing you down to the nub yet. But it got to Sam. He got to the point that he just didn't care about them anymore, I guess."

"Tell him we're thinking about him and praying for him," Ms. McDowell said.

"Yes, I will," Mr. Pippin replied, clutching his battered briefcase and bustling to his car.

Alonee sighed deeply. Her heart ached. She didn't want to believe that Mr. Buckingham was going to die because of all the cruel vandalism. She didn't want to believe that Eric Carney was behind it all because then she and Oliver would be partly to blame. Alonee hoped that Mr. Buckingham would get well and return to Tubman and that the criminal behind all this wouldn't be someone from the school.

CHAPTER NINE

Later on that Friday morning, as Alonee passed Ms. McDowell's classroom, she noticed the teacher at her desk correcting papers. Alonee walked in slowly. "Ms. McDowell . . . have you heard anything about Mr. Buckingham?" she asked.

"Mr. Pippin called and said he's in intensive care," Ms. McDowell reported. "They're still taking a lot of tests, Alonee. We're all hoping for the best, of course."

"I wonder if anybody saw anything unusual last night," Alonee remarked. "I mean, maybe someone put the box of snakes there last night. There was a maintenance man working there when I left school real late. Maybe he saw something suspicious."

"When was the maintenance man working there, Alonee?" Ms. McDowell asked.

"Around seven-thirty," Alonee said. "He was fixing the sprinklers. He said gophers were damaging the pipes. Oliver and I talked to him."

"That sounds strange," Ms. McDowell remarked. "Why would somebody be working at that hour?"

"He seemed to know Mr. Buckingham," Alonee explained. "He said Mr. Buckingham wanted the problem fixed because he hates to waste water."

Ms. McDowell frowned. "Alonee, would you come with me over to the school office?"

"Sure," Alonee agreed.

When they got to the office, Ms. McDowell asked the secretary if anyone was scheduled to fix the sprinklers behind the science building last evening. The secretary checked her records and shook her head. "No, I don't have anything here. Let me page Isaac. If anybody was doing maintenance on the campus, Isaac would know about it."

A few minutes later, a big, burly man in a denim overall appeared. Alonee recognized him as someone she saw frequently around the campus. He could repair anything. He always had a smile on his face too. "Isaac," the secretary said, "you okay a man to work on the sprinklers behind the science building yesterday evening?"

Isaac shook his head in an emphatic no. "That'd be my department. Nobody touches those pipes but me. I don't let no strange dude mess with my pipes."

Ms. McDowell said, "Alonee Lennox here, she's a junior. She and her friend Oliver noticed a man working on the sprinklers last night behind the science building."

"He said the gophers had damaged the pipes," Alonee added.

"Gophers!" Isaac cried. "We done them in years ago!" Isaac looked at Alonee. "You ever see this dude before?"

"No," Alonee answered, "but he seemed to know all about Mr. Buckingham. He even used his first name—Sam. He said he often did work for him, and Mr. Buckingham called him to fix the sprinklers because water was being wasted."

The secretary looked at her records for visitors and businesspeople who had signed into the front office yesterday. Even parents coming on campus had to sign in first. "I have no record of a repairman at all," she noted.

"He said his name was Bob," Alonee remembered. "He had this slogan, 'Get Bob for the Job.'"

"I think we need to get Bob and ask him some questions," Isaac stated.

"I suppose it's possible," Ms. McDowell suggested, "that Sam went over somebody's head and got his friend over to work on the pipes. I did notice a bit too much water on the sidewalks, but we need to look into this."

A police officer came to Tubman High that afternoon, and both Alonee and Oliver were excused from their last class to talk to him in the main office.

"We need for you to describe this man who appeared to be fixing the sprinklers," the officer began.

"He was about fifty," Alonee recalled, "and he was kinda balding at the forehead . . . and he had this little thin mustache. He wasn't dressed like a repairman. I noticed he had dress shoes on, not big work shoes."

"I agree with all that," Oliver stated. "Only thing I'd add, he raised his arm once to wipe perspiration off his brow, and I noticed he had a tattoo on his right forearm. It was a snake, and the motto, 'Don't tread on me.'"

"Oh, I didn't see that," Alonee said.

The officer asked a few more questions about the man and the truck he was driving. Unfortunately, neither of the students noted the license plate number. The officer thanked them, and they all left the office.

"That man the other night seemed kinda weird," Alonee commented, as they strolled away from the building. "I was thinking . . . I hope it wasn't Eric's father or something."

"I don't know," Oliver responded. "It's possible. He'd be about the right age, I guess. He seemed to know all about Mr. Buckingham's concern for the environment. If Eric's been complaining to his father about that teacher being so mean, maybe the guy decided to take the matter into his own hands. Eric's dad is kinda violent or he wouldn't have been beating on the kid. I'd hate to suggest that to the police, though."

"Here we are, protecting Eric again," Alonee remarked. "Maybe us protecting him in the first place caused all this trouble, Oliver. He was trying to break into Mr. Buckingham's office. We should have called the police. My dad always says if you show too much compassion to wrong-doers, then you're hurting their victims."

"Alonee, I hear what you're saying," Oliver said, his eyes narrowing. "But if we think this Bob is connected to Eric, let's find out ourselves. Let's not involve the police right away. It's so easy for a kid like Eric to be swept over into the criminal justice system. He's right on the edge, even though he didn't do anything. Then he goes to juvie, and ends up becoming a criminal just by being packed into a cell with so many delinquents."

Alonee was surprised by the passion in Oliver's voice. She couldn't help wondering where that came from. He seemed to have had an idyllic childhood. He had two loving parents who treasured him. Obviously he had no personal scrapes with the law. So what was giving Oliver that over-the-top determination to save Eric, even though Eric had a shady past and was trying to break into a locked building? He even punched Oliver in the face as he tried to escape. Where did his passion to help a would-be criminal come from, Alonee wondered?

"Oliver," she argued, "did you hear Eric today after science class? He was almost rejoicing over what happened to Mr. Buckingham. Eric was hoping he never came back. The kid has so much hatred in him. Who knows what he'll do next?"

"Well, Alonee," Oliver finally asked, "what do *you* want to do?"

"I think," Alonee asserted, "we should tell the police everything, including how he tried to break into the science building. I think we need to let them know that he violently resisted you when you tried to stop him. I think reporting things to the police would help them take a closer look at Eric, and his family, and maybe other criminals connected to them who might have done their dirty work. Like this Bob could be an uncle, a cousin—who knows?"

Oliver sighed deeply. He looked miserable. "They're a creepy family anyway, aren't they? They live on a crummy street, in a crummy house, a bunch of dirty kids playing out front, a baby in the mom's arms . . ."

"Have you been there?" Alonee asked in surprise, amazed at how well he was describing the Carney family in the green house on Indigo Street.

"No, but I know what Eric is and that's the kind of place he comes from," Oliver explained, "and we don't expect much from that kind."

"You're trying to tell me," Alonee protested, "that I think Eric is guilty because he comes from a poor background. But that's not it, Oliver. He tried to break into a locked school building. He hit you! If you hadn't been stronger than him, he might have hurt you bad. Oliver, I can't believe you don't see that."

"Alonee," Oliver insisted, "if you really believe it's the right thing to do to go to the police right now and tell them everything, then you need to do it. I'm not going to try to talk you out of it. If your conscience tells you that's the right thing to do, then go for it."

"But you don't think it's the right thing to do, do you, Oliver?" Alonee asked.

"No, I don't," he replied. "I think the kid is right on the edge of a precipice. He could go either way. If we tell the police he was trying to bust into Mr. Buckingham's classroom, he's cooked. It doesn't matter if he had anything to do with the fires or the snakes. It just doesn't matter at that point. He's under arrest for attempted burglary. Attempted breaking and entering. And that old charge against him gets dusted off and put on the table. It's over for him."

In silence, Alonee and Oliver walked to the front of the school and stopped at the statue of Harriet Tubman. She stood there, as noble as ever in the afternoon sun. There was an iron bench nearby, and Alonee sat down. Oliver joined her.

"I won't then," Alonee announced.

"Won't what?" Oliver asked.

"Tell the police what Eric did that Sunday," Alonee said. "Oliver, I have only known you for a little while, but I've grown to respect you a lot. If you feel that strongly about it, I'm going along with you. I hope we're not making a horrible mistake, but I'm going to take that chance."

"I hope we're not making a mistake too," Oliver agreed. "I'm going with my gut is all. I'm not going to pretend I'm some great judge of human nature or that I know Eric didn't do any of these things. I just don't. But I'm going with a gut feeling."

Alonee smiled at Oliver. "Good luck to us, huh?"

"Alonee," Oliver confided, "I'm going to do a little checking around on my own. See if anybody knows this character— Bob. The name was probably phony, but maybe somebody can connect the dots, if in fact the guy had anything to do with the snakes. The snake tattoo should be a help. If I come up with anything, I'll call you right away."

After Oliver left her, Alonee wasn't sure what she was feeling. She felt a little like someone walking a high wire without a parachute. She was acting on faith, faith in Oliver's judgment.

With plenty of light still left in the day, Alonee started for home. She loved to walk home at this time of day, when the sky was gradually taking on the colors of the sunset. Although the town was far from any wilderness area, there were little pocket canyons and brushy fields all around it. The small green patches provided a home for the little creatures who at one time had lived there in abundance. There were rabbits, raccoons, opossum, and skunks. Amazingly, they had found ways to survive in empty sheds, patches of brush, hollowed tree trunks. Sometimes, as Alonee walked home, a cottontail rabbit would race across her path as it scrambled toward a green lawn. Since the drought had devoured the natural vegetation, planted greenery had become their salad bars.

Something about the desperate little creatures, struggling to make it in a hostile and shrinking world, reminded Alonee of Eric. Most of the people in the neighborhood didn't want rabbits eating their gardens or opossum hanging from their tails glaring at them in the darkness. But the creatures had no place else to go. And for the most part, the world didn't want the Eric Carneys hanging around either.

As Alonee neared her own house with the rose bushes in front she was impressed by what a pretty street it was. It was nothing like Indigo Street. Almost everyone had a green front yard with nice plants. Most people had colorful flowers out front. A few lawns even sported elves and pretty pottery.

Most of the people on the street owned their own homes, though they were paying off mortgages. The Lennoxes had a mortgage. Many of the people on the street were one or two paychecks away from losing everything, but they had pretty good jobs. They were firefighters like Alonee's father, or police officers, or postal workers, or they had pretty secure blue-collar jobs. It was unusual to see the dreaded sign "Owned by Bank" go up in front of a house on this street.

The people on Alonee's street were doing much better than the people on Indigo Street.

Alonee remembered some of her many conversations with Jaris when he was mired in one of his dark moods. He would wonder how the winners and the losers in life were decided, as if somehow fate put you on one list or the other at a very early age. He would question if it happened the moment you were born or when you were in first grade or in high school. Now Alonee wondered when it happened for Eric Carney. Could there ever be any doubt that he would be one of the losers?

Nobody could really explain why some people won and some people lost, Alonee thought, but you could make little stabs at an explanation. She'd heard Pastor Bromley one Sunday trying to explain it. Pastor Bromley said that, when people experience suffering and hardship, they are better able to help others who are suffering and miserable. They learn compassion. It was as good an explanation as any, Alonee thought.

Alonee also wondered whether Mr. Buckingham had ever really suffered in his life. Was that why he had so little compassion for people? And what about Oliver Randall? Why did he have such empathy for a kid like Eric? Alonee doubted Oliver had ever stolen a candy bar or that he had suffered much, yet he had more compassion than she had seen in anyone in a long time.

CHAPTER TEN

On Saturday morning there was grim news from the hospital. Mr. Buckingham had indeed suffered a heart attack, but the doctors weren't sure yet how serious it was. He was still in intensive care.

Alonee's conflicted conscience was bothering her again. If they had reported Eric that Sunday, would Mr. Buckingham now be eating his breakfast at home instead of lying in a hospital bed connected to tubes?

"What's wrong, Alonee?" Lark asked, coming into her bedroom. "You look sad."

"Oh all that bad stuff at school and Mr. Buckingham getting the heart attack," Alonee explained.

"Did you *see* the snakes, Alonee?" Lark asked, both disgusted and fascinated by the event.

"No, thank heaven," Alonee answered.

"One time a boy brought a snake to school, his pet snake," Lark said. "He said it was nice and everything, but it made me sick."

Jolene and Tucker came into Alonee's room too. Tucker lay on the floor and played with his Transformers. "Did they leave any more snakes at your school, Alonee?" Jolene asked, giggling.

"No," Alonee replied.

Tucker listened to some of the conversation and then announced, "I *like* snakes. Snakes are awwwesome."

"You would," Jolene said, rolling her eyes.

"I'm gonna get a snake," Tucker declared.

"No way," Lark objected. "Not in this house."

Tucker did a somersault on the floor. Then he said, "I saw a man with a snake."

Alonee was fixing Jolene's hair with ribbons when she stopped suddenly. "Did he have a real snake, Tucker?" she asked.

Tucker waved his arm in the air and pointed. "His snake was right here."

Alonee finished Jolene's hair and knelt on the floor with Tucker. "Was it a picture of a snake on the man's arm, Tucker?"

"Yessss," Tucker said.

"Where did you see this man, Tucker?" Alonee asked.

"In the store," Tucker answered.

"What store?" Alonee asked him.

Tucker did another somersault and said, "I dunno."

Alonee rushed into the kitchen. "Mom, when's the last time you took Tucker with you to the store?" she asked.

"Yesterday," Mom said. "We stopped at the Ninety-Nine-Cent and More store. Why?"

Alonee went into the living room, where her father was watching an old rerun on television. "Dad, would you drive me to the Ninety-Nine-Cent and More store right now?" she asked. "It's really important."

Floyd Lennox smiled at Alonee. "Sure, baby. Anything for my girl. I can always get something there myself. It's much cheaper than in the supermarket."

In a few minutes Alonee and her father were driving toward the 99¢ and More store. "Baby," Dad commented, "your mother says all her friends like that boy you're going with. They all hear good things about him. Oliver seems like a fine young man. When the womenfolk like a boy, that's a pretty good thing."

"He's special," Alonee said.

"You are too, Alonee-Dolly," Dad told her.

Alonee first went to Derrick, who worked at the store. She asked him if he had ever seen a man with a snake tattoo on his arm in the store. Derrick looked thoughtful, then he shook his head no. "Don't think so. Maybe my boss has. Wes! Would you please come here a minute? My friend is asking about a guy with a snake tattoo on his arm."

Wes came around the corner of the beverage aisle. "Hi Alonee," he greeted. "How's the family?"

"Good," Alonee said. "Do you remember seeing a man in the store with a snake tattoo on his arm?"

"Oh sure," Wes replied. "He comes in all the time. He's new in the neighborhood. First came in about a month ago. Comes in here and buys beer and cigarettes mostly. I saw the snake tattoo and the saying, 'Don't tread on me,' and I asked him what it meant. He said it meant no dude better lean on him, or he'd be sorry."

"Do you know his name?" Alonee asked.

"He told me his name was Joe," Wes answered. "His brother-in-law and sister own an apartment building over on Algonquin. He told me they got terrible financial problems. Seems like the government has come down hard on them for some violations. Joe said they might lose everything. I told him I feel for him. Governments are corrupt. We lost everything we had over in Iraq. Had to start from scratch here . . . I guess governments are the same all over."

"Thanks so much, Wes," Alonee said. Her heart was pounding so hard she could hardly breathe.

Mr. Buckingham lived on Algonquin Avenue.

"Dad, could we drive over to Algonquin?" Alonee asked.

"Sure baby," Dad agreed. "What are we looking for? Is this a scavenger hunt?"

"Dad," she explained as they were driving, "I think the man who lives over there had something to do with the fire at Tubman High and what happened to Mr. Buckingham's car and the snakes too."

Alonee had once visited Mr. Buckingham at his apartment. He invited a few of his best students to the roof to view the planets from his expensive telescope. He and his wife lived in a front apartment with deep red curtains. Alonee had met Mrs. Buckingham during that visit and again at school.

They parked in the visitor's area, went up to the Buckingham apartment, and rang the bell. Mrs. Buckingham answered the door. "Mrs. Buckingham," Alonee asked before making introductions, "how is your husband?"

"He's doing a little better. I'm going over there now," she replied. "My son is driving me."

"This is my dad, Mrs. Buckingham." Alonee said.

Mr. Lennox shook hands with Mrs. Buckingham, and said, "We hope we're not disturbing you, ma'am. But Alonee feels she can help find the man who burned your car."

Mrs. Buckingham's face showed interest. She turned to Alonee and inquired, "You're one of Sam's students, aren't you? We've met once or twice."

"Yes," Alonee said and then went on, eager to explain the reason for her visit.

"I'm trying to help the police find out who did all those terrible things at school and to your car. There was a man at our school the night before the snakes were left outside your husband's classroom. The man had a snake tattoo on his arm and the motto 'Don't tread on me.' I was wondering if you—"

Mrs. Buckingham cut into Alonee's words, a terrible look coming to her face. "Joe Alwyn," she said. "That terrible, ugly man. He's been staying across the street. His brother-in-law is Gary Wister, the man Sam made all the trouble for. Wister owns that apartment across the street. He was dumping pollutants into the storm drain, and my husband called the authorities. The hazmat team came out and—oh, it was awful. Wister and his wife were cursing us." Mrs. Buckingham clutched herself and rocked back and forth. "It was a nightmare. I begged Sam not to call the police. Now the Wisters are going to have to pay huge fines. They're losing everything and blaming us."

"Oh my gosh!" Alonee cried. "Mr. Buckingham told us in class how proud he was of turning in the criminals who were fouling up the waterways."

"I begged him not to do it," Mrs. Buckingham continued. "I almost got on my knees and begged him, but Sam is a fanatic when it comes to the environment. I think he would lay down his life to save the spotted owl. Do you think the Wisters and Joe Alwyn are responsible for the school fire, burning our car, and the horrible snakes?"

"Well," Alonee began to answer. She looked questioningly at Dad, who nodded a yes to her. "We're going to the police right now. They've got evidence from the fire and the box of snakes. If Joe Alwyn is involved, they'll get him."

"Thank you for talking to us," Alonee's father said. "Mrs. Buckingham, you and your husband are in our prayers."

"Thank *you*," Mrs. Buckingham replied. "Perhaps at last this terrible nightmare will be over."

As Alonee's father drove her to the police station, she called Oliver. "Oliver, I think we know who set the fires and brought the snakes to school. Remember when Mr. Buckingham was bragging in class how he turned his polluting neighbor over to the cops? Well, the guy with the snake tattoo who said his name was Bob is the brother-in-law of the guy Mr. Buckingham brought down. Dad's taking me to the police station right now. I'll call you when I get home."

"Wow!" was all Oliver could say. "*Wow!*"

The officer in charge of the investigation wasn't at the station. Alonee left a handwritten statement for him and signed it.

When they got home, Alonee called Oliver again. He came over to her house promptly. When he came into the living room, he shook hands with Alonee's father and gave her mother a hug. "You've got a fabulous daughter," Oliver told them. "She means a lot to me."

"So I've heard," Alonee's father said.

Then Alonee and Oliver went outside to the little gazebo, accompanied by pieces of Mom's pumpkin pie.

"You did quite a piece of police work, girl," Oliver told Alonee. "I think congratulations are in order."

Alonee laughed. "Actually, all the credit goes to my little brother, Tucker. He said he saw a man with a snake on his arm in the store, and it was easy from there. The only place Mom recently took Tucker was the Ninety-Nine-Cent and More store, and Wes knew right away who the guy was. Of course, we're not sure yet that these people are the culprits. But it sure looks like that's what that guy was doing there when we saw him—not fixing the irrigation pipes, but dropping off the snakes!"

Oliver nodded.

"So that means Eric *was* innocent, huh?" Alonee remarked.

"That would be the case, yeah," Oliver agreed.

"Oliver, then I would have to say you were right, wouldn't I?" Alonee said.

"Well, you could say that if you wanted to," Oliver replied, with a half smile on his lips.

"Because except for you," Alonee said, "Eric would be in jail now for trying to break into that science building. He'd be in terrible trouble."

"I guess so," Oliver said, eating his pie.

"You know, Oliver," Alonee continued, "what really puzzles me is how you had so much sympathy for the guy . . . almost as if you'd been through something like that yourself."

Oliver finished his slice of pumpkin pie and put his fork down. Mom looked out the door and said, "Want seconds? You're a growing boy, you know."

"Yeah," Oliver called, "thank you!"

"You haven't answered my question, Oliver," Alonee persisted. "Where did all that passionate defense of Eric come from?"

"Well," Oliver began to explain, "when I was small, my father used to read me Shakespeare's plays. One day he read *The Merchant of Venice* to me. I remember this one line . . .

The quality of mercy is not strain'd,
It droppeth like the gentle rain from heaven.

"You mean, Oliver," Alonee responded, "that a pretty quote from Shakespeare changed your life and gave you all that sympathy for the underdog? Is that what I'm supposed to believe?"

Oliver laughed. "No, no. It was something else my father told me that did it. My father lived in this rough neighborhood in South Central, and he joined a gang when he was a boy. It wasn't a gang like we have today. There weren't drugs and drive-by shootings, but the kids tossed clods of dirt at passing cars, and they stole fruit from the outdoor markets—that kind of stuff. Well, one night Dad and his rowdy buddies had

176

climbed on a roof. Dad was about fourteen but big for his age. The kids were trying to get down into a closed store, but the cops showed up. They shined their searchlights on the kids, and they came down and gave up. Not Pop. He made a run for it. He came down from the roof and sprinted down an alley. He was a good student, and he was scared about what his parents would say if the cops arrested him. My father ran down that alley like the wind with a cop after him, a white cop."

"Oh brother," Alonee groaned.

"In those days the white cops weren't too thrilled with troublemaking black kids," Oliver continued. "Anyway, my dad tripped over something. He fell down in the alley. He had a flashlight in his hand. It was very dark. My dad started to get up with that flashlight in his hand, and, well, the flashlight looked just like a gun. So here's the cop with his gun out, and a big black kid is getting up and he's got a gun. At least, that's what it looked like to the cop."

"Oh my gosh!" Alonee gasped. "The cop didn't shoot him, did he?"

"He almost did," Oliver went on. "In that split second the cop made a decision—a decision that could have cost the cop his life. He screamed *"Drop it!"* instead of shooting, and my father dropped the flashlight. The cop could have lost his own life because he didn't want to shoot a kid. A lot of people might say the cop did something stupid, and in a way he did. But he showed mercy. With his own life on the line, he showed mercy. That cop, we found out later, had a wife and little kids, and he risked all that."

"Oh man," Alonee gasped.

"Anyway," Oliver kept saying, "he drags my dad up by the scruff of his neck and throws him in the patrol car. He yells in my dad's face for ten minutes and says he almost killed him. He calls my dad a stupid idiot. My dad was crying. He told the cop he was a straight-A student, and he never did anything really bad in his life, and now he wouldn't

even steal fruit. The cop drives my father home and shoves him in the front door. He tells my grandparents, 'I never want to see this punk again on the roof of a building, or in an alley, or pinching apples.' "

Oliver smiled then. "When my father graduated high school, his parents sent that cop an invitation. My dad was valedictorian. The cop came. When Dad graduated college, magna cum laude, the cop got another invitation . . . and he came. He shook my dad's hand. When my dad began teaching at the university, he and my dad golfed together. They became close. And then, when my dad heard that the cop had died, he was one of the pallbearers at his funeral. See, Alonee, except for that bold-hearted act of mercy in a dark alley, my dad might have died at age fourteen, and, well, all this now would have been different, right?"

"There never would have been an Oliver Randall for one thing," Alonee mused. "And that would be a major tragedy."

"And I wouldn't have been here to show mercy to Eric," Oliver added.

Alonee leaned over and gave Oliver a big hug that lasted long enough to get the attention of Alonee's parents, who told them that it was time to come in.

"Getting too chilly out there," Mom called.

"Getting too hot out there," Dad protested.

Alonee and Oliver came inside.

On Monday, Gary Wister and his brother-in-law, Joe Alwyn, were arrested for arson and for acts of harassment and violence, among other charges. Alwyn's fingerprints were found on the snake box, and the reptile dealer identified Gary Wister as the man who bought the reptiles. Both men implicated the other when the evidence began piling up. Gary Wister had committed petty crimes in the past, but his rage against the neighbor across the street who set the cops on him was so

intense that he wanted to destroy Mr. Buckingham.

"That old fanatic ruined me. Everything I worked so hard to earn, he took away from me," Gary Wister wept.

On a rainy Friday night, Oliver sang at the junior-senior talent show at Tubman High. He sang John Legend's "Ordinary People" and brought down the house. Alonee clapped until her hands hurt, and all his friends told Oliver he had stopped the show.

But it was a grungy looking boy backstage who made the night for Oliver Randall. Eric Carney clutched a test in his hand. "Dude," he told Oliver, "the substitute teacher, she said Buckingham's getting better in the hospital. He'll be back but not right away. She gave me the makeup test old Buckingham had left. That lady who took his place, she gave me my test back. I got a C plus, man. First time in my life I ever got a C plus in science!" His eyes gleamed with hope.

Oliver reached out and high-fived Eric. Then he tugged him into his arms and gave him a bear hug.

A few minutes later, as Alonee and Oliver were about to leave the auditorium, she stopped him just inside the big double doors.

"Oliver, you were right," Alonee admitted.

"Right about what?" Oliver asked, still savoring the fun and excitement of the evening.

"About Eric," she replied. "You were right to believe his story, to give him the benefit of doubt."

Feeling a little uncomfortable, Oliver blew off the compliment. "Ah, I'd rather be lucky than smart, as my dad says sometimes," he chuckled with a smile.

"Well," Alonee persisted, "lucky or smart, you were right. I learned a big lesson from you. Thanks."

"No charge," Oliver replied, still trying to keep things light.

"But you know what I hope?" Alonee went on.

"What's that, baby?" Oliver responded.

"I hope," Alonee wished, "that Mr. Buckingham learned a lesson too. That would be something great coming out of something really horrible."

"Well," Oliver replied, suddenly moved by Alonee's words, "I hope so too, babe. You know, that quality of mercy, you just never know when it's going to show up."

They kissed good-bye and hurried through the doors to the cars, where their parents were waiting to take them home.

Outside the auditorium, the rain was falling gently.